POLTERGEIST GIRL

A Savannah Nights Story

J.R. Froemling

Published by The Great Yarn Dragon, LLC

ISBN: 978-1-957393-23-0

Even in the darkest of moments, love will save you.

You do not stand alone.

This book is dark and deals with taboo subjects.
If you ever feel like all is lost, please ask for help.

TABLE OF CONTENTS

CHAPTER ONE

Ringing In The New Year

January 2, 2019

My heels click on the pavement as I approach the pack of men lounging around their pickup trucks and motorcycles. They're rugged, calloused, beautiful specimens of the male species. I love watching them work in their tight fitting blue jeans and tank tops with flannel shirts and ball caps. They're nothing like the pretty boys I went to college with, not like Richard either. These men are all manners and muscle.

The click of my heels on the pavement draws their looks up like dogs hearing a phantom whistle and a ghost of a smile graces my cherry red lips. With each precise step, I'm thankful my sunglasses hide any hint of the truth. Today, I want to be the perfect doll all the men stop to ogle. I want Richard, my fiancé, to see how lucky he was.

"Mornin' fellas," I drawl to keep the shaky hints of distress out of my voice.

I spent a full hour this morning inspecting every curated piece of clothing in my closet; Versace and Armani pressed and hung to allow me the illusion of choice. All are Richard's choices.

How many times had he told me how perfect the uncomfortable and tight skirt made me look? How many days had he caught me in the elevator to pop the top button and allow my cleavage to be on display for all the world, despite my feelings on the matter?

I chose his absolute favorite blouse. The shimmery material teases the onlooker, giving them the illusion they can see what lies beneath. I pair the soft blouse with a pin-striped pencil skirt, altered to fit the curve of my hips, stockings with seams, down to shiny black stilettos.

I spent a second hour in front of the mirror to guarantee my make-up looks effortless yet accentuates every feature God gave me. Smokey eyeshadow hides the dead-to-the-world feeling behind my eyes. Cherry red lipstick under shiny lip gloss, gives the pouty illusion of begging for true love's kiss. My blond curly hair is in a high ponytail that would rival Ariana Grande's.

Every painstaking moment of my pre-show prep is worth it as the men shift and watch my every move toward them.

"Mornin', Miss G," they chorus back as they take the donuts and coffee I come bearing to woo them to my cause.

"Where's Billy?" I ask as I pout, hoping he hasn't decided to meet me at the auction. He's not the kind of man who can hide, being well over six feet tall, all muscle, and a twinkle in his eye.

As if he hears me ask, he pulls into the parking lot. The rumble of his truck mixed with the loud country music grows louder like fanfare in a parade until he pulls into the spot his crew always leaves open for him.

I blink away the tears threatening my make-up and straighten myself to prepare for the mountain of a man. Time crawls as I wait for the truck to come to a halt. My heart hammers in my chest and my stomach twists in fearful anticipation.

Billy steps down and shares some cordial greetings with his workers. "Miss G." He drawls in greeting. I could listen to this man read the phone book.

"Hey Billy. You got a sledgehammer handy?" I clasp my hands in front of me, and work to keep my voice light and airy, like I had asked him what time it was. My palms sweat, and the muscles between my shoulders tightens as the tension builds. I hope he doesn't grill me on why I want a sledgehammer.

Billy studies me before quirking an eyebrow. Without a word, he shifts his gaze from me to his men. Without a word, they shrug and continue devouring their breakfast.

My heart is going to burst from my chest as anxiety tightens like a corkscrew. It takes all my focus to keep my breathing steady.

He eyes me up and down again before he nods and heads to the trailer hitched to his pickup.

As he rifles through it to find the tool, a genuine smile blooms on my face and I lean against the truck to unclasp my designer heels, leaving them and my purse on the ground. I can't believe I'm going to do this. A heady rush of adrenaline counters the swelling dread telling me not to. Wolf whistles chorus up from the boys as I use the excuse of straightening my skirt to wipe the clamminess from my palms. I should be more concerned about being lady-like and all prim and proper. All that has won me is the misery searing through my heart like an exploding volcano. I bounce on the balls of my feet as Billy returns with the giant slab of metal atop a yellow handle.

"Thank you."

The hammer is heavy in my hands as I heft it up onto my shoulder, and turn to face the victim my anger and frustration; a cherry red Lamborghini parked straddling a white line, forcing a buffer zone between it and nearby cars. The license plate reads "6DICK9".

I should have known. There were always signs. My chest tightens for a different reason with each step I take closer to Richard's baby. My fiancé's baby. The same damn fiancé that claims to love me and swore to me I was all he ever needed. The same one that gave me lip service in respecting my wish to save myself for marriage.

I met Richard Mahoney in high school after my father summoned home from boarding school. We were the all-American dream team. He was the starting quarterback, and I was the captain of the cheer squad. We reigned as prom king and queen for both Junior and Senior years. The rage in my father's face when I abandoned going to Yale to follow Richard to Stanford had not deterred my blind love.

College is where things took a turn for the worse. There had been one positive thing to come from that, though. That was where I met Gracey. She was my roommate in the dorms Freshman year. Blue hair, exotic tattoos and an infectious, bubbly personality was all it took for me to know we would be friends forever. Richard had never liked her. The two always seemed to fight like cats and dogs anytime they were together.

I love him so much, that tears start to well at the corners of my eyes. I gave up friends for him. I changed my clothes for him. I followed him to the school of his choice and spent four years making excuses for all his poor behavior. Love blinded me to how terrible Richard is for me. All those nights in college where we were supposed to go on a date. He claimed he was too busy studying.

Studying anatomy with everyone except me, more likely.

The heft of the hammer in my hands as my manicured fingers tighten on the fiberglass handle roots me in the present. Each time I tried to express how I felt, or tell him my dreams, he would always turn the conversation to him. He always made sure I knew my place was by his side. I wanted someone to love me so much I lost myself in being Richard's girl. He even made the grand gesture of proposing in front of all our classmates at graduation.

The night after our graduation, he took me to a swanky restaurant, and we enjoyed every wine on the list. Richard almost claimed my virginity until Gracey crashed the party and resulted in flaring up the ongoing battle between my desire to save myself and his desire to claim me.

It always ended the same way, with him belittling me and leaving me a rejected mess. Fight after fight, he whittled me down until I decided to give him what he wanted. We were engaged, and were going to get married.

This past summer, before coming to work full time for my dad, I came up with the perfect plan. We would spend the summer after our graduation backpacking across Europe, with the last weekend before coming back to the States in Paris. It was going to be magical, romantic, and the night I lost my virginity.

Instead, it was a nightmare. Richard refused to go to Europe with me. My homecoming was welcomed with crude remarks and insinuations that Gracey and were lovers.

I wanted the Richard I fell in love with to come back to me. I missed the man who would show up at random hours of the night to steal me away for endless conversations under the starry sky.

Christmas brought the best opportunity to win Richard over. We had been working together for a few months, becoming the power couple of Belmont Real Estate. After spending the minimum required amount of time with my father in the morning, I rushed home and changed into a large velvet bow, covered by a trench coat. When I arrived at his apartment, I let myself in and crept into his room.

I walked in to see Tracey, his assistant, giving him the exact Christmas present I had in mind. She was riding his North pole like a stripper. He was surprised, not ashamed, to see me. I was such a fool for believing he loved me. That's what love does to a girl like me.

My hands tighten around the hammer, frozen with the fear of his wrath. There is no going back once I make this choice.

He fucking lied to me.

He chased after me and begged my forgiveness. Showered me with promises of never again and how he loved me. That love lasted until the New Year's Eve party our company hosts.

I grit my teeth, hating his car, the one true love in his life. I pull that sledgehammer up above my head like a demented She-Ra, Princess of Power, and bring it down with all the might of my tiny five foot four frame. My scream of frustration echoes across the parking lot at all my mighty swing accomplishes is bouncing off the bright red hood, leaving a minor scuff.

I ignore the cries of "Oh, damn," that come from Billy's crew.

I heft the hammer back up and am jerked to a halt by an unseen force; the hammer plucked from my grasp. Whirling around to vent righteous wrath upon whatever was stopping me, I come face to chest with Billy Coeh.

Billy holds the hammer as if it weighs nothing.

I stamp my foot and hold out my hand, expecting the weapon back. Embarrassment threatens to steal the wind from my rage-fueled sails as the guys chortle while watching this melodrama.

"Miss G, if you keep swingin' like that, all you're gonna do is hurt yourself.".

I tense, thinking he's going to pick me up and carry me away before I attempt anymore damage. Instead, he puts his hands on my hips and turns me to face the car. Before I can stop him, he steps behind me and places the hammer in my grasp. He slides my left hand up the shaft and grips my right at the base as an anchor.

"Let physics do the work for ya. One smooth stroke." He runs my hands along the shaft of the hammer before stepping back and to the side, watching with a mirthful grin.

My cheeks flare to life and my blush runs down my neck at our precarious position. I marvel at how much lighter the hammer feels perfectly balanced between my hands. I nod at his encouragement and turn back to the car to let out a battle cry of victory.

CRASH!

The hammer slams down and leaves a most satisfying dent in the hood. My chest heaves as I struggle to breathe and giddy joy floods through my system.

"How could you?! Fucking TRACEY?!" I scream at the car.

CRASH!

The hammer shatters a headlight. I pull back, letting the burning in my arms push me on. Images of Tracey pawing and clawing at Richard flash through my mind.

"You fucking prick! I love you! Why am I not good enough?!"

CRASH!

Another dent spots his hood.

"I gave you everything! EVERYTHING! And yet you FUCKED Tracey, Carrie, and AMBER!"

Gracey had been the one to tell me last night. She caught them at the New Year's party we had thrown at work. Some may even call it the proverbial straw that broke my heart.

I sink to my knees, my shoulders shaking with the heart wrenching sobs I can't control; the foolish love-sick girl wronged in the worst way.

The car alarm blares in protest to its mistreatment.

My stomach is in knots. I've made a spectacle of myself.

Billy's gentle voice penetrates my meltdown. "Miss G, can't have you kneeling on the ground like this. It ain't lady-like. You'll ruin your stockings, and that won't do."

He scoops me up, and I curl into his arms, shielding me from the judgmental eyes I know are watching. Tears stain my cheeks and I bury my face against his chest like a small child. The few moments it takes to move from Richard's car to Billy's pickup are like floating in a dream.

Billy opens the passenger door and delicately places me into the seat. "You stay here, Miss G. We got you." He leans down and grabs my heels and purse to place them in the cabin with me. He closes the door, then heads back to the Lamborghini, picking up the forgotten sledgehammer and flipping it in hand, like it weighs nothing.

Every single one of his crew grabs an implement of destruction and within a few minutes, the cherry red car is a smoldering pile of scrap metal. The alarm wheezes out a last breath before falling silent. Not a single word transpires between the men as they then gather the breakfast I brought them, and load into their vehicles.

Movement from floor-to-ceiling windows of our office catches my attention as I lean my head against the window. They're lined with the gophers, the women from the cubicles in our office that always pop their heads up for juicy gossip. I may not see their faces, but I can see the imaginary lines being drawn between team Georgie and team Richard.

Even with Billy whisking me away, I know there will be hell to pay back to the office, either from Richard or my father. Richard for the car, and my father for the scene. He hates public drama. I could use a stiff drink and wonder if Gracey will want to party tonight.

Billy pulls me from my misery by reaching over and patting my knee. "Don't worry, darlin'. You'll be alright. You're too good for Dick anyhow. 'Sides. We gotta get to Haven Hill for the auction."

CHAPTER TWO

The House That Love Bought

"Miss G?"

I crack an eye open as I side eye Billy from where I lean against the window. The rumble of the diesel engine comforts me, like a purring cat. I'm safe here. Billy would never let anything happen to me. His wife, Shelley, has made it clear on more than one occasion she threatened his manhood if he did. I always love talking to Shelley at company get-togethers. She may be tiny, like me, but she's the boss between the two of them.

"Yeah?" My voice is raw from screaming and crying.

"We're ten minutes out. Shelley keeps a touch-up kit in the glove box. I'm sure she won't mind you borrowing it."

Billy's ever thoughtful and sweet. Jealousy stabs me through the heart as I sit up and flip down the visor to check my appearance.

Dark streaks cut channels down my cheeks and lipstick is

smeared from where I had wiped away the snot. I reach for the glove box and work to touch up the destroyed make-up.

Billy waves a hand at me when I try to apologize for ruining his handkerchief. The damn man digs into the center console between us to fish up fresh wipes.

By the time we turn off the highway onto the plantation's drive, I have managed to remove the proof of my emotional devastation and pseudo-hide the red blotchy patches.

The run-down plantation house looms in the distance and there are dozens of cars parked on the spotty lawn. An auctioneer's platform is set up to the far side with chairs laid out in rows before it. People wander in and out of the open house.

Haven Hill is going to be my show-stopper project. This house has been here since the Civil War, and most people want to snatch it up for the land since it isn't too far from the interstate. I, on the other hand, love restoring houses to their former glory. My eyes scan the assembled crowd and my breath hitches when I see Richard standing next to his mother.

That explains why he wasn't in the office. He's going to help his family buy this place out from under me.

When Billy parks, I pop the door open and slide around to let my feet dangle. I slide the heels back into place and regret my choice of footwear as I step onto the uneven ground.

Billy has already come around the truck, and I give him a quick hug to steady myself as well as thank him for his help. His embrace is warm and comforting, and I wish I had someone like Billy to hug me like this all the time.

His brow quirks at the sudden, odd sign of affection before his gaze follows down to my body. A small smile forms on his lips and he offers his arm to help me until we get to better ground.

Richard's eyes bore into me the entire walk to the registration desk.

To which, I ignore him. Instead, I study the Victorian architecture of the house. The wrap-around porch has a high roof line and imposing white columns supporting it. Extra tall windows line both floors of the house, giving insight into the massive size of this place. My eyes dance across all the little details that have weathered the years of storms blowing through this city.

"Hey there, Georgie. Glad you could finally make it." Richard's playful jab gives away his displeasure. He has a fake smile plastered on his face. His glance darts from me to Billy and back, accusing me of some indiscretion without saying a word.

When he leans in to kiss me hello, I turn my cheek and shift my weight away from him. "Why aren't you at the office? I'm the one who handles auctions for Belmont Real Estate." Any other day, I would be terrified of upsetting him. Fretting at even bringing up the slightest inconvenience to him as it would somehow be my fault. I want him to confess his crime of working for his mother today.

My gaze levels on Mrs. Mahoney, hovering like a vulture waiting for the roadkill to quit breathing. The first time I met her was in high school. We had been dating for some time. He always managed to find an excuse to come to my house until I put my foot down. My face hardens and my back stiffens as I meet her eyes.

Her lips form into a sneering smile and I lift my chin, daring her to say something to me.

Richard tries to canoodle up with me.

I slip his grip and dance to the other side of Billy. He provides the best shield against Richard's radiating anger of my silent rejection. I walk with Billy, laughing and talking as if I hadn't spent the morning in tears.

Richard doesn't believe in consorting with peasants like Wolf Pack Construction.

Billy's hand rests on the small of my back to usher me into the house.

Richard's face hardens.

A triumphant smile blossoms on my face.

The inside of the main house eradicates all thoughts of my awful morning. A large, grand staircase curls up and splits into a balcony over the main floor. Music, men in suits and top hats, and ladies in silky ballgowns dance in my head as we enter the ballroom. The oak floors are worn down and dirty. Dust leaves a gray film over every surface. At least nature has been kept at bay.

I can't decide where to look first with all the details and finishes.

"Billy, this place is amazing."

I run my hands along the wainscoting, loving the sound of my heels as they click against the oak flooring. The two of us walk through the house, and my fingers dance along every nook and cranny I can find.

We pass through a set of double pocket doors.

"Oh. My. God." I turn to Billy and squeal. "This place has a library."

From the first time I watched Beauty and the Beast I wanted a castle with a library. Not a room with some bookshelves in it that a person calls a library. No, a proper library with built-in shelving lining all four walls and a rolling ladder to reach the upper levels.

"This place is a death trap," Mother Mahoney hisses.

My hands wave and I'm animated as I point out all the things

I want to keep, or refurbish, ignoring the awful woman.

Billy's amiable smile and enthusiastic encouragement only adds to my excitement. When we reach the back of the estate, there is a massive stone porch that leads down into what used to be gardens. The weeds and shrubbery have grown over the fountains. All I can is the potential this land has.

All of the bidders are ushered to the auction area.

"Georgie." Richard says.

I brush by him as I head to my seat.

He has the gall to sit next to me, followed by his mother next to him.

I white knuckle the hem of my skirt to resist changing seats.

"Bidding starts at five hundred thousand." The high-pitched voice of the auctioneer is hard to understand through the crappy speakers.

"You know, Richard, this area will make for a wonderful shopping district and condos." Mother Mahoney lifts her paddle. "Two million, and let's be done with it."

My blood boils at the idea that this beautiful, history-rich estate will be bulldozed for shopping and condos. I relent my cold shoulder treatment and give Richard the attention he has been seeking this morning with a beguiling smile and a shift to face him.

"I really want this one, Rich." I lean in, giving him a perfect peek down my blouse, and bat my eyelashes at him. "Please?"

He swallows hard as his eyes are frozen to my chest. I trail my fingers down his arm in how Gracey had shown me.

"Two-five!" My call is crystal clear as I raise my paddle with the other hand.

Richard stiffens.

"I know you do, darlin'." Richard stage whispers at me. "This place will take every bit of twelve to do it any justice. Plus, can you imagine what it would cost to run utilities this far out? Mother will keep the charm of the main house. The Historical Society will make sure of that."

"Three." Mother Mahoney calls out.

My back goes ramrod straight and I frown. His mother is not getting this house if I have to sell all my worldly possessions to get it.

"Three Five," I chirp.

"Five," Mother Mahoney snarls.

The rest of the bidders have fallen to the peanut gallery to watch the two largest firms in Savannah duke it out. Mother Mahoney stares daggers at me, waiting for the auctioneer to declare her the winner.

"It'll take twelve?" My voice holds a serene, sweetness as I relish the tense uncertainty in Richard's eyes. "Twelve!" I exclaim with a flick of my paddle.

"What are you doing?" Richard grips my wrist and hisses.

I jerk my wrist free and my sweet smile turns to a vindictive grin. "I'm buying a house at auction, Richard. Maybe you should have checked with Carrie and Amber to make sure Tracey got you the memo about this being an auction."

Richard's flinch brings a blossom of elation in my adrenaline-fueled madness. His eyes cut between me and his mother, as panic replaces any traces of anger he had before.

Ice water is thrown on my elation as Mother Mahoney's shrill voice cuts through the air, "Twelve-five."

I don't hesitate as my hand leaps back into the air. "Fifteen million."

"Twenty".

Richard's body bounces as he shifts back and forth between

the two of us. The blow of me revealing my knowledge of his indiscretions causes him to sputter.

"Twenty-five," I say with confidence. This property isn't worth more than eight at most, and I'm well aware the Mahoneys don't have this kind of money thanks to Richard's lamenting.

"Hey, Mother, Georgie. Wouldn't this make an amazing wedding gift? The merging of the two firms? Everyone working together to revamp and rebuild this area."

Richard's words are met with wilting gazes from both of us.

"Fine. Thirty-five million, split between Belmont and Mahoney." The woman spits the words at my feet.

How dare he try to claim this bullshit now. The other bidders turn in their seats, anxious to see how this telenovela plays out.

My finger rubs the smooth void where my engagement ring was. I had left it in his apartment this morning before I went home to get ready for work. He should have changed the locks after I found him with Tracey.

"Thirty-five five, Belmont alone." I watch the auctioneer, not wanting to look at Richard's handsome face. This is what his love has done to me. Driving me to rage-buy a dilapidated mansion for more than five times what it's worth.

The mix of murmurs and gasps fill the lawn.

CHAPTER THREE

The Next Time He Cheats

"Sold! To Belmont Real Estate! Congratulations, Darlin'!"

The gavel bang thunderclaps in my ears like the cannon in the 1812 Overture. In my scorned woman high, I agreed to spend an absurd amount of money. My father is going to kill me. The thrill of making Richard suffer has worn off and shock sets in. I stare at the auctioneer, who's smiling at me, unable to breathe.

"What in the fuck have you done?" Richard grabs me by the arms and lifts me from my chair, forcing me to look at him. A vein bulges on his forehead, and his cheeks are blotchy red, like mine when I've been crying.

I giggle, a nervous and unhinged little sound at how comical his face is in perspective of how far-fetched my revenge has been.

Richard has never been violent toward me, and I have no reason to fear him. The grip on my forearms and the blazing hellfire in his eyes ceases all giggling, replaced by a whimper.

"You destroyed your father's company, you dumb fucking cunt! I shouldn't be surprised. You've never been fucking good at business. I don't know why your father insists on you being in charge of auctions. Obviously, you're too dumb to handle them." His voice is pitched low.

"Richard," I beg, no longer wanting to make him suffer as I have. What was I thinking? Each venomous word lashes my battered heart.

He pulls me closer, leaning in until I feel his hot breath against my cheek while he continues his onslaught. "All you fucking care about is your petty vengeance. There. You got it! Are you happy? We're all out of a job now. How you could fucking think I would ever marry you is beyond me. You're pathetic."

He releases me as if I scorched him, and it causes me to plop back into my chair. My cheeks flame red, my lips part, and my vision blurs with the tears threatening to elude me again.

Richard turns his back to me and walks away with his mother.

Those nearest to us gasp and the whispered judgment roars louder than my screams as I destroyed his baby. I turned my personal life into a spectacle for all the world to see. My lip quivers as panic and sadness battle for control. My father doesn't have that kind of liquid income sitting around.

Despite wanting to fall to pieces and blubber like a small child, I keep my composure. I have to find a way out of this, to fix our broken relationship, and to pretend like today never happened. Richard will forgive me if I save the company. I want to run to the auctioneer and explain there was a terrible mistake.

Billy's massive form appears in front of me and he squats down to get to my eye level.

"Miss G, I think you should take this call," his voice is coaxing, like he is with his youngest child, and his hand rests on my knee giving me a light shake.

I blink like an owl at the outstretched phone. The caller ID reads "Savannah Historical Society" and I watch the call timer tick like a stopwatch in a race.

"Huh?"

"Miss G, trust me. You're gonna want to take this call." He waves the phone at me.

Taking his massive tablet he calls a phone, I bring it to my ear. "Hello? This is Georgina."

"Hello, Miss Belmont." The voice on the other end of the line is smooth and calm. "This is Mehzebeen from The Savannah Historical Society. I believe you just purchased Haven Hill Plantation for quite a sum of money."

"Uh-huh," is the only response I can muster, like a small child being talked out of a tantrum. Mehzebeen is one of my father's oldest friends. The rumor mill spins with stories of a long-standing tryst between them.

"The Savannah Historical Society has a vested interest in preserving landmarks such as the Haven Hill Plantation. We are willing to partner with Belmont Real Estate in an equitable agreement. You get to renovate the estate and put your mark on it. The Historical Society gains a new event venue for fundraising and cultural education. Of course, we would require the estate be preserved. We will take the steps necessary to have the land declared a historical landmark to prevent future sales for prospective developers. If you are amenable to a fifty percent partnership I-."

"Yes! Oh, yes! I would love to work with you." I cut her off without listening to the rest of the deal.

Billy's megawatt grin greets me. He pats my knee and stands

back up.

Her crystalline laugh is like the calm after a hurricane. I can draw in air, and my shoulders relax. Nothing can repair the wounds to my heart. But I haven't doomed us all to destitution.

"I appreciate your cooperation, Miss Belmont. I will instruct the auctioneer to amend the contract. You, however, must be the one to tell your father of our arrangement."

I hand the phone back to Billy after the other woman hangs up. The bubbling energy of having a way out of this mess triumphs over the battlefield of my love life. I leap out of my chair and wrap my arms around Billy's waist, needing a hug more than anything.

"I didn't ruin us!"

"Of course, Miss G." He laughs with me as he pats my back.

Billy, while not being family, is like a brother to me. He listens to all my drama, gives advice, and teases me. He always comes through on the projects and he's the ever steady mountain my whirlwind of crazy rails against.

I breathe easier as I head up to deal with the paperwork, able to ignore the hollow pit in my stomach. It takes two hours of back-and-forth negotiation before we get the contract settled. Belmont Real Estate would be in charge of the actual construction and overall design and aesthetic. The Savannah Historical Society will have the final say on approving any changes. After completion, both companies will own the property, and neither can sell it without the other's consent.

The focus required to complete the auction purchase allows me to forget the drama that started before the sun came up. As we walk back to Billy's truck, I realize I have not looked at my phone once this morning. I fish it out of my purse and blanch at the number of missed text messages.

My chest tightens and my heart pounds in my chest. The urge to hug myself and rock like a Weeble-Wobble threatens to paralyze me as I stare down at my phone.

"Everything alright, Miss G?"

No, of course everything isn't alright. I've committed two felonies today and took my father's company to the brink of ruin. What kind of question is that? "I'm fine," I squeak out. If any of those messages are as hateful as Richard was I will shatter, so I stuff my phone back in my purse.

Billy offers his hand for me to help me into the truck, and I shrink into the passenger seat. The desire to go home and hide under a fuzzy blanket for the rest of my life the leading contender in my bad-decision drama. Regret crashes into me like a tidal wave of ice water. Goosebumps race down my back and arms. Oh no, I've ruined everything.

Richard was furious, but he never mentioned his car or apartment.

I'm going to jail.

This morning before work, I detoured to Richard's place. He always goes to work before me.

I let myself in with the key he gave me.

The fancy butcher knife he is so proud of being signed by Bobby Flay was my weapon of choice. It sliced through his leather furniture and mattress as if they were butter. His over-priced cologne went down the drain. Ketchup and mustard decorated every suit, shirt, and shoe until there was no amount of OxyClean to repair them. I took a nail file to all of his Xbox and PlayStation games. I shattered his television with his Xbox before I dumped both gaming consoles into the sink and left the water running. The piece de resistance of my Waiting To Exhale moment was leaving my engagement ring on his mantle above his fireplace.

Destroying his apartment was not enough. I wanted him to suffer as much as I am. To feel his entire world being ripped from him and to know it was me who took it all from him.

How could I do all these things?

I curl more into the seat, hugging myself tighter. Billy keeps stealing glances at me. Fear grips me like an over-synched corset. I'm convinced the police are waiting for me at the office, ready to haul me away.

"Billy?" My voice is small and I worry he may not have heard me over the roar.

"Yes, Miss G?"

"Is there something wrong with me?"

"No, Miss G," he says with a chuckle.

The finality in his voice brings me comfort. I should be able to turn to my father for this kind of advice. Any conversation I have with him ends in shouting. He hates I exist.

"Did I screw up?" Icy dread gnaws at my heart as I await Billy's verdict. Billy's disapproval might be the final stake in my chest to send me into a total mental breakdown.

"You definitely made a mess." He shrugs. "But here's the thing 'bout messes. They're only messes iffn you don't clean 'em up. You made a choice, now you gotta deal with the consequences. You had to do what was right for you, and for what it's worth, I got your back."

"Yeah. Okay." I reach for my purse to call Richard. I will apologize. He'll understand. We'll move past my behavior.

Billy's hand rests on mine, preventing me from getting to my phone.

"Let it be. You take this time to put yourself together. You are gonna need that strength when we get back to the office."

CHAPTER FOUR

Young Love Murdered

As difficult as it is to not pick up my phone to launch a forgiveness campaign, I listen to Billy. I look out the window to enjoy my last minutes of freedom. My mind has other plans and replays the morning on repeat. How I could have gone to Richard and begged him to not cheat on me. That I will be better, and we're perfect together. How I've put him in this awful situation, and everything he has been forced to do is my fault.

I only realize we are at the office after the truck stops.

The parking lot is empty. No wreckage. No cops. No Richard. The empty spot where Richard's car had been this morning is pristine. Like the car never existed. Had I imagined the whole thing? I slide my oversized sunglasses in place.

Billy waits, not pressuring me to hurry up.

"Thanks, Billy."

"Ma'am." He bobs his head. "If you need anything, I'm a call away. I mean anything."

"I will. Thanks again."

I draw in a deep breath before I open the door and slide out of his truck to face the music. The walk of shame into the office reminds me of my first day of school here in Savannah. Everyone staring and judging the new girl. Inside the glass doors, I stop. The urge to turn tail and run for Canada is strong. I could start over. My dad would send me money. If he won't, Gracey will. As I turn to start my life as a fugitive, I see Gracey barreling toward the door.

Sophia Grace Halburton-Minsk III, Gracey to her friends, is a tall woman with blue hair and spiraling tattoos covering her body. Today she shines in a purple dress with Mary Janes. She plows into me and engulfs me in a bear hug.

On instinct my arms clamp around her and I bury my face against her. The mix of sea salt and caramel surrounds me and protects me in a comforting cocoon. No matter how terrible my life gets, Gracey makes it better.

"Georgie, thank God!" She pulls back and holds me at arm's length, inspecting every inch of my body. "Why haven't you answered my texts?"

"I was busy," I mumble in a lame attempt at a defense.

"Nuh-uh. You don't get to ignore my text messages on a day like this. Why didn't you tell me? I would have made sure Dick was watching the entire time while I helped you do it!" She whispers to me.

I blink in surprise. She is my ride or die. Hearing her antics aloud makes my heart sing. I give her a tight smile and shrug. She's trying to perk me up. There was no way I could have involved her in this. Richard being mad at me was one thing, Gracey is another. He would send her to prison for what I did to punish me faster than I can blink.

"It's fine, Gracey." I hug her again before extracting myself to face my father. "I need to talk to Dad about the new project before anyone else does."

"Really? We're going to pretend it didn't happen?" She slips back in front of me blocking my path to the elevator.

"Yup. That's exactly what we're going to do."

"Georgie." She wags her finger at me. "I admit, I never expected you to trash his car. I'm so… proud of you."

Her smile is infectious.

"It wasn't just his car," I whisper, biting my lower lip as I smile.

"Wait, what? Oh, Georgie, what did you do?"

Out of any other person, that question is an accusation rife with condemnation and judgment. From Gracey, it's a genuine child-like glee of a toddler ready to wreck their parent's home.

"I…" I glance around and pitch my voice so only she can hear. "I redecorated Richard's apartment."

Her laugh is gregarious and rich as she doubles over.

"It's not funny! Gracey!" I swat at her arm to get her to stop as the elevator dings open.

"Yes, yes, it is. It's fucking hilarious!" Gracey wipes tears from her eyes as we step into the elevator. "Anyway, I'm proud of you Georgie. That'll teach him."

The mirth of Gracey enjoying my reckless behavior is short-lived. The doors whoosh open on the fifth floor, and we step out, all conversations stop and the Gophers peek over their walls. A reckoning is coming, and my feet are weighed down like they're in cement. It's stuffy and hot in here. I can't breathe. No police officers in sight, is a relief.

"Are you going to be alright?" Gracey asks.

"Yeah, I'm fine."

She nods, gives me another quick hug, then she's off to deal with a commotion on the far side of the floor, near the break room.

I make a B-Line for my office, avoiding my father's office, dealing with any of the Gophers, and hoping Richard isn't waiting. The bright room is as muted as a confessional booth. Richard's desk is supposed to be on the right side. Only the indents in the carpet remain. My desk sits in the center of the space, facing the door.

"Oh no," I whine. Did they get rid of Richard? Did my outburst this morning cause my father to fire him? Is this why everyone is playing the quiet game behind me? I step forward and set my purse on my desk, followed by my sunglasses.

"What! The! Fuck!" Richard's voice roars from across the office.

I whirl around.

He's red-faced, and his suit askew. Nothing like how he was at the auction a few hours ago.

My heart cries at seeing him in such distress.

He closes the distance between our offices like a stampede of wild horses.

"There you are, Saint Georgina! The virgin fucking martyr! I am your goddamn fiancé! If you didn't want to marry me, then why the fucking hell did you take that piece of shit ring?! If you have issues, why didn't you come talk to me, like a civilized person?"

Alcohol and stale sex invades the small office as he barges in and pushes himself right into my face.

I stumble back and we dance this sadistic tango.

"You are one dumb fucking cunt! You and those inbred Coeh

fuckers! Once I'm done with you, you'll be rotting your rich princess bitch ass in a federal fuck-me-in-the-ass prison!"

I shake my head no at him. He hates me. All I wanted was for him to love me. Why couldn't he see that? All I wanted was for him to need me. To be enough for him. He's right. How could I do all this to him? Why didn't I talk to him? Why did I have to fly off the handle?

"I," deflating under his menace. "I'm sorry."

"Sorry?! You're fucking sorry?"

My back hits the window.

He forces himself into my bubble.

I turn my head to the side. My body trembles as I brace myself for him to hurt me. I deserve this.

"Does that mean you admit you did something wrong?" His voice is low and threatening as he presses his nose against my cheek.

I gag from the stench emanating from him.

"You don't get to hang your head and pout like all you did was break a few toys. You meant to hurt me. You succeeded. Happy? Is this what you wanted? For me to be forced into the arms of other women? For me to torture myself with these needs and desires? I wanted you, but you said no. I asked you, but you said no. I waited for you, but you never came. You finally decide 'Oh, I guess it's okay', then you want me! Then you come to me!" His hand slams against the glass window.

I yelp and bring my hands up between us to protect myself.

"This is fucking bullshit! I do everything for you, and this is how you treat me!"

Fight or flight causes any markers I might have had left for the day to be tossed aside. I did this to him. I destroyed a man and made him a monster. All I ever wanted was for someone to love me. I was too unreasonable to ask him to respect my faith and wait until we are married. Tears stain my cheeks again, and I'm trembling from my efforts to not incur Richard's wrath further.

He chuffs like an angry dog and shoves away from me. "Fuck this, Georgie. Give me my key."

I dare to lift my gaze at his words and the cracks of my porcelain strength grow wider. Long gone is the sweet boy from high school.

Contempt rolls off him like the stench of his sexcapades as his stormy green eyes remain leveled on me.

Trying not to sob in front of him, I hiccup and sniffle, my lip quivering.

He keeps his gaze on me as he paces like a caged beast.

With trembling hands I fumble getting my keys out of my purse and dart fretful glances to see if my fear will set him off again. The several tries to remove the key cause my hands to shake more.

He stops in front of me, the desk the only thing between us.

"I…" my voice catches as I cannot stop a hiccup. "Hope you find someone who is worth everything to you. Your spare suit is in your office. You should clean up before Dad sees you." How did it end up like this? All I wanted was for us to be happy.

I want him to take it all back and be my Richard again. To pull me into his arms and apologize for everything he said this morning so I can forgive him. To not smell like sex and booze, reminding me I am not enough for him.

He stares down at the key like a wild animal being lured into a trap before he snatches the key and shoves it into his pocket.

My hand curls back around the purse, and my face burns hot in shame. I always overreact. I will rot in prison because I couldn't behave like a civil human being.

"Both of you. My office." My dad growls from the entryway. "Miss Halburton-Mensk, I require an HR representative."

We freeze and our eyes meet. How long had my father been standing there? What did he hear? What will he do to Richard, or me?

Fearful Richard might still attack me, I don't move until he does.

Gracey pauses me at the door of my office, extracting my purse from my clutches and walks alongside me, guiding the last prisoner to the trial of my life, my father the iron mountain judge. Each step grows harder, and my skin burns with how silent the office is as we are paraded to my father's office.

"Close the door." He commands. My dad stands at the window, his back to us, his hands clasped behind his back, reminding me more of a super villain in a Bond movie.

Gracey steps past me as she walks to stand in the corner next to him. Her hand brushes along my arm, offering silent encouragement with a light smile.

Richard snorts and throws himself into the chair.

I lower myself onto the edge of the other seat, forcing my hands to uncurl and lay flat against my skirt and cross my legs as the ankle like I had been taught.

My father says nothing, and doesn't move.

Gracey clicks her pen and opens her folio, sitting in the corner, poised to take notes.

She's in HR mode and as much as I want to fling myself into her arms and cry this out, I have to be professional. My father doesn't tolerate this kind of tomfoolery in his office. The longer the silence lingers the more I feel the sword of Damocles over my head, threatening to plummet at any moment and put me out of my pathetic existence. I steal a side glance at Richard. My lip quivers. I pushed him yet again into the arms of another woman. I wring my hands and shift, trying to remain composed and failing. I can't take it. I can't be the reason my fiancé is fired. After everything, I can at least take the fall and save Richard's job.

"Daddy, please don't be mad at Richard. This is my fault. I wanted Haven Hill. It's a lot of money. Richard tried to stop me. That's why he's so angry. But I have enough to cover part of it on my own. I can get investors for the rest-"

My father raises a hand to cut me off without turning around. "I don't know the details of what happened between you two. I don't want to know." His words are graveled and strained. "But this is a place of business, and you are partners in it. You two blew every other team out of the water by ten percent last quarter. I cannot afford to lose either of you. The Belmont Real Estate Corporation requires the utmost professionalism."

My breath catches as he turns. His jaw twitches and his dark eyes bore into Richard, then me. No softness, no understanding. All he cares about is his company and image. Another failure and another reason for him to hate me. My hands curl, and I death grip my skirt as I shrink back into the chair, wanting to turn invisible.

"One of you cheated. One of you got carried away with a hammer. I don't care."

I gulp and open my mouth to defend Richard.

His eyes snap to me and furious anger gives him a dangerous and menacing appearance.

I close my mouth.

"If the two of you want to continue playing War of the Roses, fine. Pack your boxes and get out. This is an office, not a frat house. On my time you will conduct yourselves with the utmost dignity and respect." He steps forward, leaning on his desk for emphasis. His knuckles go white from the pressure and the wooden desk groans under his menacing weight. "If I hear so much as a peep of any unprofessional behavior," he shifts his glare to Richard, "you will both be out on your asses faster than you can blink. Do I make myself clear?"

"Yes, sir." My voice is soft and the words are muted.

"Yes, sir." Richard's voice echoes mine.

"Good, Richard, get yourself cleaned up and get back to work. Gracey, please continue overseeing the office migration."

Richard shoots out of his seat as soon as my father releases him, slamming the door behind me.

I flinch.

Gracey pauses on her way out and gives my shoulder a gentle squeeze before she follows Richard.

CHAPTER FIVE

Thank You For Being a Friend

I wasn't dismissed and I'm not tempting fate by angering my father further, but I'm not strong enough to keep from crying again. My hands shift to hugging myself and I stare at my knees, too afraid of seeing another person I love hate me today.

"Georgina." The gravel in his voice is off-putting after his stern reprimand. He fishes out a small handkerchief and passes it to me.

The small cloth smells of his cologne and longing aches in my chest. Why did it have to be this way? Why does every man in my life hate me? What's wrong with me? I want nothing more than to fling myself into my dad's arms and for him to promise he'll fix everything. Instead, I struggle to keep my back straight, struggling to remain professional and strong.

"What's going to happen to me?" My voice cracks, and once again, I'm the little girl being taken to London and abandoned with the Van Helsing family because my father hates me.

"Everything is going to be fine. I took care of it."

The shift in my father's tone causes my head to snap up and stare at him. He rubs his hand over his face and the weariness peaks through the iron curtain.

"What do you mean, 'took care of it'?" Did he do something illegal? Are we're both going to have to flee to Canada, the Belmont name ruined?

"Richard will be fine. You will be fine. No one's going to prison, and no one's getting fired."

Was that a joke? My life's falling apart and he chooses to mock me? I am pathetic.

"What happened at the auction?"

His chair creaks as he settles into it. I give the handkerchief a few more twists before looking up to him. His brow is arched, and he's leaning back in his seat, casual, and calm. Like he asked me what I had for breakfast, and not my rash attempt to financially destroy the company.

"Please don't be angry, Daddy. I-."

He holds his hand up. "Stop. You made the investment already. How much?"

"Seventeen."

His dark eyebrows draw to the center, forming a crease between them and he turns his head to the side, as if he's calculating in his head. "I was told Haven Hill went for thirty-five, five. Care to explain?"

If he knew what happened at Haven Hill, why is he asking me? Was he trying to catch me in a lie? I purse my lips together and stare at my father trying to figure out what he's doing. Is he going to take this away from me? Or worse, give it all to Richard?

"I couldn't let her win, Daddy. Mrs. Mahoney wanted to turn it into condos and shops, demolishing the entire place. I was angry, and Richard tried to stop us," my voice falters at the mention of Richard and tears well in my eyes again.

My father tenses, "I can imagine."

The fire in my belly flares at assuming he's taking Richard's side over mine. "Hrmph. I'm telling this story."

"My apologies. Please continue." He waves his hand like the king allowing the peasant to air their grievances.

"I was trying to figure out how to scrape together all that money. My plan was to cajole investors, make deals with the devil, maybe even tap out my trust fund, when Billy hands me the phone. It was Mehzebeen, from the Historical Society, and she offered to partner with Belmont Real Estate and put in half the costs." I pause as a dark look twists over my father's face before the iron curtain pulls his emotions out of reach.

"In agreement for renovating and not demolishing, we would have the site dubbed a historical landmark, and use it for the benefit of both companies."

"Really?"

"Really. That was the only requirement for her to share the bill with us."

Suspicion clouds his face.

I hold my breath as I try to figure out what I said wrong. I thought he would be ecstatic. I managed to make the biggest deal of my life.

"I'll reach out to Mehzebeen and finalize the contract. However," he points at me, "as your punishment I am using your trust fund as collateral for the loan. Any overages to the budget will come out of your pocket. The company will not go a penny over what Richard approves. Is that understood, young lady."

"Thank you, Daddy! I promise. I won't let you down!"

"Don't thank me yet. You still need Richard's approval for your budget."

The lead stone knots in my stomach returns with a vengeance and I scrunch my face, like I sucked lemons.

His face softens. "You're going to be alright, Georgina. Next time, let's avoid criminal activity when expressing ourselves."

"Yes, sir," I murmur, studying the front of his desk instead of looking him in the eyes.

"I believe you have work to do."

How am I going to make nice after destroying everything Richard owns? I stand outside his office, his door clicking closed behind me, frozen by indecision. That is until the Gophers pop up to watch. I refuse to let them dictate my life here, or to let them see how broken I am. I lift my chin and walk as calmly as I can muster to my office, shutting the door behind me.

I reach over and press the button that lowers the blinds, shielding the office from view. As much as I would like to run home and hide, I have work to do. The first task of this project is to declare a truce with Richard, and hope he will forgive me enough to not tank this project.

Detouring into the private bathroom for our, no, my office, I take a hard look at myself in the mirror. Between the repeated crying jags and the cheaper make-up Shelley Coeh keeps, there are puffy bags under my eyes, shadowed lines from wiping away tears, and one hollow, dead-inside girl no one will ever love. I shake my head to fling those morose thoughts away and get to work. I remove my blouse and wash my face, removing the emergency touch-up work. Once assured Richard will work with me, I'm going home, anyway. No one will see me that long.

With my blouse secured and buttoned, I fuss over the rest of my outfit to return myself to the perfection that is Georgina Belmont. On the way to Richard's new office, I pause at the break room and snag a white napkin. Unfolding it, I follow the workers still moving furniture into his office, only stopping at the door to wave it before entering.

"What do you want, Georgina? Come to gloat?"

"Richard, I," but I stop, as I don't know what to say, or how to move forward. What if I say the wrong thing and he yells at me again?

The men moving his filing cabinets are the only sounds between us in this room. This was a conference room prior to this morning. While I get the view and the airy windows, he gets much more space.

"Leave it and get out." He barks at them.

"Losing my temper was unacceptable. I will pay for whatever insurance doesn't cover."

He stops with the rustling of papers on his desk and looks at me. "You know what, Georgie? No. Keep your money. I'll figure it out."

The fire burning in his eyes forces me to turn my attention to the napkin in my hand that becomes the most fascinating piece of tissue in the world. "If you need a place to sleep… My apartment is available." I add to clarify, "I can stay with Daddy."

When he doesn't respond, I look up.

He's staring at me with his mouth agape and his eyebrows raised high.

"Georgina, I'm not staying at your apartment. Is that all you needed?"

"No." I sigh and shift my weight. I never thought it would be this difficult to talk shop. "Daddy says we have to work together on Haven Hill. I will get you my proposed budget by Monday." My lip hurts with how hard I bite it to keep from launching into a plea to not be angry and how I didn't tell my father he slept with anyone. Realizing now that my father already knew, and I was the only fool here who didn't.

"Whatever. Just get it on my desk. I'll make it work. Is that all?"

Not trusting myself to say another word, I nod and flee back to my office. I pack my briefcase and snag my laptop in record time before I dash to the elevator to escape today. Alone in the mirrored box, I stare at the desperate doll no one will ever love. I'm pathetic and don't deserve happiness.

The elevator dings and whooshes open, revealing Gracey waiting at the front desk holding her own purse and making small talk with the security guard. She breaks off and struts my way.

Despite how awful I feel, I smile.

"What? Did you think you could skip out of work without your HR manager knowing? Don't worry. I informed your supervisor I would see you home and guarantee no employees will further harass you today." She flashes a devilish grin as she links arms with me.

"My supervisor?"

"Your old man, duh." She rolls her eyes as she pulls me towards the front door. "No more moping. What are we doing tonight to celebrate?" Gracey veers me away from the crime scene to her tiny mini coup, not giving me a chance to answer as she fills me in on what the Gophers did when I destroyed his car. Once we're settled in, she turns in the driver's seat and asks,

"So… his apartment?"

"Yeah, his apartment."

She cackles with laughter, like a cartoon villain. "Tell me you took pictures!"

"No," I mutter. "Why would I take pictures?!" I smile at her antics.

"Phooey." She juts out her lower lip and gives me doe eyes. "Think we could get there before Dick does?"

"You did see how mad he was, right?"

"I sure did! Silver lining, since there are no photos, he can't prove it was you."

"That's not how this works. How any of this works." I wave my hands around like the woman in the commercial.

"Uh-huh. Where do you want to go?" She turns to start the car.

"Home. To forget everything that happened today."

"Then it's my choice?" Gracey lights up like a small child let loose in a candy store.

The last time Gracey decided our destination, we ended up in Amsterdam. We started that day in Italy. She still hasn't told me how we got there.

"I promise we'll stay in the greater Savannah area." She crosses her heart with one finger.

"Uh-huh." No matter how bad I feel, Gracey always cheers me up. Pulling my seatbelt on, I'm able to relax.

She drives like the devil himself is chasing us to my apartment. Her melodious voice provides a constant patter. Where we are going. What we're going to wear. The best drinks they sell. How many hot dudes she wants me to bring back with me.

Everything is going fine until we get into my bedroom-sized closet. I freeze in place. The long line of pencil skirts and silk blouses hang like cloaked judges at the trial of my love life. I sink to my knees and sob.

"Awe," Gracey mewls and pulls me into a bear hug. "Shh, it's alright. Let it all out." Her arms cradle me close and she pets me like she would a kitten, cooing to me and rocking me. She lets me sob in her arms until I'm reduced to hiccup-laced sniffles. Then she pushes me to arm's length. "Girl, you are a hot, fucking mess. First things first, get naked."

"Gracey," I whine.

"Second," she continues undeterred, "go and stand under those amazing fucking power washers you call a shower until all evidence of Dick is gone."

I huff and cross my arms.

"Third. Sweatpants and comfy shirts only." She wags her finger at me. "One that isn't his! Then, and only then, do you get to make the most important life-altering decision of your life." She pauses for dramatics.

As much as I want to remain in my depressed pity party, I giggle at her antics. "What, pray-tell, is this life-altering decision?"

"Cookies and Cream or Cherry Garcia?"

"Cherry Garcia, always." I mock salute and bust out laughing as Gracey reaches for my tucked-in blouse.

"You're not getting naked fast enough."

CHAPTER SIX

Bagels of Regret

Gracey's body sprawls across my king-sized bed and for such a tiny woman she takes all the available space, turning me into her personal pillow.

Europe brought us closer together, and we spent many a nights canoodle in places much smaller than this as she spent the Summer trying to make me forget Richard. Tonight rivaled that excess from pizza to candy, then ice cream and wine as we laughed our way through Ghastly Renovations.

My mouth's dry and my head pounds. Gracey performing her best blanket impersonation. I run my fingers through her hair as I stare at the ceiling.

Richard never understood my closeness with Gracey and spent every opportunity to remind me what a terrible influence she is on me. Richard often accused us of being inappropriate together. Sure, Gracey's forward. She has never been shy about her preferences. Gracey doesn't discriminate when it comes to enjoying herself with men, women, or anyone else. Not once since the day I met her has she crossed the line.

With Gracey, I can be myself. I can laugh at stupid jokes. I can wear whatever I want. There's no fear I will say the wrong thing, or embarrass her. Is that why he hates her? I've always tried to include him. It ends the same way; with him getting drunk and picking a fight with her, forcing me to separate the two of them.

Would that mean I'd have to give up my best friend if he takes me back?

I shift my gaze from the ceiling to the sleeping woman on top of me. My chest aches at the idea of having a life without her. She's funny, kind, and carefree. She's my only confidant I can tell everything too. Richard only listens until I've irritated him with my inane chatter.

I squirm until I can roll on my side and face my nightstand. My phone is right there. All I have to do is reach out and I can text him. I can explain myself and ask his forgiveness. He always forgives me. It may take a few days. Every fight we've had before goes the same way. We fight. We break up. I come crawling back.

Gracey grumbles and doubles down on claiming me as her pillow when I reach for the phone. Warmth radiates from her and my body relaxes, causing me to hesitate in making what she would call a mistake. Snuggling into her grip, the heaviness of sleep lulls me and I decide to leave dealing with Richard for in the morning.

My phone chimes with the text message notification and my eyes fly open.

Is it Richard? Is he apologizing for how hateful he was to me? I hate myself for knowing if he even utters one apologetic word, or inkling of kindness I will forgive him everything. That's what you do when you love someone. We'll go back to how it was before and I'll be happy. I creep my fingers along the side of the bed until I can grapple my cell phone while keeping my eyes on Gracey. I don't want her to wake and catch me. Guilt causes me to breathe faster, knowing that having to sneak means I shouldn't be looking. It proves how pathetic I am.

My covert mission to retrieve my phone succeeds. The screen lights up. A selfie of Gracey, Richard, and me blooms to life of us wearing orange life preservers and holding brightly colored double-bladed paddles. White-water rapids rage behind us. We all have such beautiful smiles. What I wouldn't give to go back to that trip.

You up?

Yeah. Can't sleep.

I clutch my phone, the three dots taunting me as he types. The mix of excitement and fear makes my stomach churn. What if he is still angry with me? Or he's pressing charges? What do I do if he tells me to lose his number?

Wanted to say sorry. I was out of line today. Can you forgive me?

I exhale. Re-reading the sentences to verify he's apologizing. Instead of enjoying the moment, anxiety tap dances across my brain, sending me into a mental tizzy. He should be mad. He should be angry. Why is he saying that he was the one out of line? Was this some kind of game for him? I scour every centimeter of the screen trying to decipher what that short, brief message means.

"Georgie, you're an idiot. Tell him to fuck off." I whisper. "He's the prick who cheated. You destroyed all his stuff."

I huff.

"Which you regret. He's offering an olive branch. Maybe he realized how close he came to losing me and is willing to change?"

My eyes squeeze shut as I let the scales weigh out my feelings. Anger and hurt balance against my need for love and fear of abandonment.

I sigh as I type my response. I will always forgive him. That's what it means to love someone.

Always. I am so sorry for being such a terrible girlfriend.

Will he take me back? I wriggle free of Gracey and pad across the hardwood floors into the en-suite bathroom. Closing the door behind me, I sink to the floor to stare at the screen in the harsh bathroom light. I have to know. Does he accept my apology?

I know. I forgive you. Seeing you in such a state pains me. Let's talk over coffee in the morning.

I catch the phone before it can hit the floor as it slips from my numb fingers. He accepted me! He's willing to talk it over. I delete the first three versions of the response where I accept without hesitation. Yes, he was willing to forgive me, but he still hurt me. Apprehension chews my insides up like an alien trying to birth itself. I can't just take him back. He cheated. How can I go into a marriage with a man who won't even respect that sanctity?

I don't think that's a good idea, Richard. What if I upset you again?

My heart is in my throat again as I watch the bubbles dance. Minutes pass like days while I watch the screen, needing to know his response. What if my response makes him angry again? How will I face him at work if he's pissed off all the time? God, how will I ever face him again? I have to set the device on the floor and stare at the bland white bathroom ceiling to keep from bombarding him with follow up apologies.

Memories bubble to the surface. Our first date at a co-ed party with twinkle lights and a bunch of horny teenagers playing spin the bottle. Our first sweet kiss in the dank basement closet. Inviting me over to help him with his homework as an excuse to watch movies in the media den of his home. Endless hours lying in my bedroom chatting with him until the sun rose. My torment ends with the small chime from the phone.

It will be fine. Six?

Hope flutters in my heart. Can start from scratch and erase all this bullshit between us? I would give anything for Richard's hateful gaze and stinging words to be bleached from my memories.

Perfect! I'll be there. Love you.

Love you.

Pure blissful energy floods through me as I mad-dash to prepare myself. It was already five in the morning and I needed a shower, make-up, clothes, and to order a ride. Richard hates to be kept waiting.

For a date like this, I would spend hours primping and making myself perfect. I don't agonize over my outfit, instead grabbing everything that I know Richard likes. The pink lacy bra and panties match my 'Perfectly Bashful' lip gloss. The blue blouse and pin-striped pencil skirt with stockings and heels complete the outfit.

I pause and watch Gracey sleeping still, having replaced me with my pillow again, and I make sure to set her phone alarm before bolting out the door. If I wake her, we're going to fight about caving in again and that's the last thing I want.

The entire ride to the coffee shop I check my phone and urge the driver to go faster. The Uber drops me off with a minute to spare. I take three seconds to straighten my clothes before drawing in a deep breath and heading into the shop.

Richard is already there and waiting with two cups of coffee. He stands as I approach and rakes his eyes over me, a smile dancing over his lips. A gentle kiss and a tight hug tells me everything is going to be fine.

"I'm sorry for the way I behaved yesterday. Thank you for giving me another chance."

The Jekyll and Hyde that is Richard Mahoney stuns me into sitting in the chair he pulls out for me without question. I can't believe it. He heard me and is willing to fix the mess I made. The tingles that run up my arm from his light touch remind me how much I miss him.

"What are your plans for today?"

I study him as I sip my hot cream with a dash of coffee. He's treating this like any other workday morning. The niggle of doubt comes crawling back like the living dead bursting forth from the cemetery of terrible thoughts. What if he doesn't want to get back together? Did he call me here to build me up so he could shatter me in public? Was he about to destroy me like I destroyed his car? I use the hot cup in my hands to buy time to get my emotions in check.

"I was going to take today off, but I have two houses on the East Side I need to look at. Billy's picking me up at seven-thirty to head to the first one."

The flash of anger that burns across Richard's face would have been easy to miss if I weren't watching for it. Was he jealous of every person in my life that wasn't him? He's going to have to get over that if we are to continue. I love all the people in my life and want him to love them too.

The background noise of the coffee shop is the only sound

between us. I roll my shoulders, working out the knot forming between my shoulder blades. Using this as my excuse to reach for the bagel sitting in the middle of the table. I focus on the delicious pile of carbs as I meticulously spread cream cheese on it and avoid Richard.

I can't take the silence and try to fill it. "I was also planning on clubbing after work."

"You always have enjoyed dancing. Mind if I tag along tonight? Is Gracey going with you?"

My lip twitches and nose scrunches for an instant in surprise. I look over at him through my lashes as I gauge his reaction. Richard hates clubbing. Why is he asking to go? Does he want to spend time with me? What's his angle? Especially if he wants to go with Gracey there. They mix like oil and water.

"Probably not. She has an HR thing this week. I'll have to text her."

I shrug and take a healthy bite of my carby goodness.

"Great!" He bumps the table as he bolts up from the chair. "Gotta go see how much of the budget you didn't follow for the condo on Maverick." He gives my cheek a quick peck.

Then he's gone. No hug. No lingering, soulful goodbyes. No 'you hang up first'. I eye the bagel in my hands. I spend the next few minutes savoring the morning delicacy and then fish out my phone. Gracey should be up.

Wake up! 🐦 Dick wants to go. 7 pm?

I don't even have time to watch the bubbles dance when her response comes through.

Yup. Meet you there. Why are you talking to Dick? :(

Sweet! Let's go to Onga Bongo. Smoothing ruffled feathers. Have to work together, remember?

CHAPTER SEVEN

Dancing Queen

The day is spent out of the office. Billy ushers me from house to house, showing the progress on each project. He repeats himself more than once. All I can think about is tonight. He never scolds me for being distracted, or ask what's going on. The other guys keep acting weird, though. They keep approaching me, open their mouth to speak, look at Billy and excuse themselves without saying a word. I decide to leave well enough alone, as they're still getting work done.

Tonight must be perfect. The right dress, maybe some ecstasy, as I show both Gracey and Richard that we can all exist together. I'm not going to screw this up again. We're going to dance the night away. If all goes well, we'll remember why we fell in love.

Every time my little brain goblin rears his ugly head to say I'm a fool and I should kick Richard in the balls, I punt him back into the depths of my subconscious. Even my father wants us to work through our issues.

Tonight I need Richard to see everything he could have; the wild and untamed me. I curl my hair and finger comb it. Glittery eyeshadow and "Sinful Berry" lip gloss shine in the light. In the back of my massive closet hangs a red sequined dress. I was saving it for Valentine's, but this is an emergency.

At six forty-five, I exit my building to see Richard leaning against a shiny new car, a wet dream come to life in slacks and a dress shirt left unbuttoned at the collar.

His gaze roves over me and he shifts his weight before giving me a smoldering smile. "You look lovely," he drawls.

"Nice upgrade." I whistle to him as I run my fingers along the side of the car, beaming at his compliment.

"Yeah, it's the latest model. Just came out. It's only a rental, so try not to dent this one."

His tone is playful, yet a dagger rips through my heart as he reminds me of my actions.

I keep the smile stuck to my lips and continue to circle it. He loves cars. He put the best part of a hundred miles on the Lamborghini showing it off to me. The door hisses to life at the press of a button. He is the perfect gentleman as he helps me into the low riding car.

From this vantage point, there is little to the imagination in my outfit. He hums and licks his lips before he closes the door. Seconds later, we are racing across town to Onga Bongo.

Richard knows the drill for clubbing nights. He pulls the car into the valet stand, tosses the man the keys and a twenty. I latch onto his arm, excitement building at the faint call of the music. The bouncer with a clipboard never bats an eye as the two of us walk past him. I make sure to give him a wink and an air kiss in thanks.

The bass thumps its tantalizing call to join the packed dance floor. From wall to wall, the young and beautiful let go of all their cares to let the music move them. I breathe easier. All I need is to enjoy myself and making sure Richard never wants to leave me again.

My eyes gravitate to the center of the dance floor. Gracey's head is down and her hands are high above it. Her blue hair is braided with sparkling jeweled clips, and her purple dress hugs her body like paint on a canvas. The men around her grind and groove to her beat as they all jockey for her attention.

Lifting her gaze, our eyes meet, and we both smile. The urge to join her grows stronger as Richard leans in to brush his lips along my ear.

"I'll get the drinks."

I nod and let him lead on, remaining by his side instead of giving in to Gracey's alluring invitation.

We balance a flight of shots each as we make our way towards a booth in the back. It's occupied until Richard slips them money, causing them to vacate and leave us alone.

I roll my eyes at his show of money and desire to hide in the furthest corner from the dance floor. My first shot is sweet and burns all the way down. Before Richard can take his first off the tiny tray, I snatch it from him.

"Nuh-uh, mister. You want this shot? Then you're going to have to earn it."

I pop the entire shot into my mouth. The smoky flavor of the whiskey he ordered is heady and rich. I crawl up into his lap and wrap my knees around his waist. Not pausing to give myself time to chicken out, I drape my arms over his shoulders and lean into him.

His body rages like an inferno against me as he stiffens.

I want his lips on mine, to taste the sweet mix of alcohol and Richard. My heart races as his hands dance over my back and butt. Excitement stirs and heat blooms between my legs as I feel him stir beneath me. This is what I wanted. I wanted him to want me. Not Tracey. Not Amber. Me. I shift my hips down. The hard bulge in his pants rubs against me and makes my heart beat faster. His eyes are only on me.

I lean in, intent on shot-gunning the whiskey into his mouth when my phone goes off. The ringtone is loud enough to pierce through the nightclub. I squeeze my eyes shut and groan internally. Why did it have to go off now? I swallow the whiskey and sigh.

Richard's grasp on my ass tightens, and he peppers my neck with kisses. "Just ignore it. Tonight is you and me, baby." His voice is thick with lust and his raging hard-on teases me.

This is the moment I know he has dreamed of for years. He's begging me for more, and I want to give him everything. We're going to be alright. He's going to love me. My phone rings a second time and I deflate, fishing it from my purse to check the caller ID.

"Richard, it's the police! I have to take this!"

I don't give him time to respond as I shoot off his lap and push my way to the ladies' room to find a quieter place to take the call. "Hello."

"Miss Belmont, this is the Georgia State Patrol. We are calling to let you know there has been an incident at Haven Hill. We need you to come verify nothing was taken."

I stamp my foot in frustration. It's like even the universe doesn't want us to get together. I order a car and hurry back to where I left Richard.

"I'll be right there," I mutter into the phone and hang up.

Gracey is at the booth, and it looks like the two of them are arguing again. I can't play referee tonight. It never ends well when the two of them are arguing. Gracey hauls off and slaps Richard hard enough his head snaps to the side.

"Gracey! What the fuck?!"

My shout causes both of them to turn and face me. The daggered stare on her face transforms into a bright smile as she sees me. I push myself into her space, anger boiling up.

"Apologize this instant!"

"What? No! You're too good for this prick and he doesn't deserve this second chance you're giving him." She crosses her arms and huffs.

"Gracey. Apologize." I cross my arms and stare her down.

She huffs before turning to face Richard. "Sorry for slapping the shit out of your lying ass face." Sarcasm and disdain drip from every word.

Richard opens his mouth to speak, and I snatch their hands, cutting him off.

"Please. I have to go. Something's happened at Haven Hill. You two play nice and make up, okay? I love you both. So, please, for me." My eyes dart between them, willing them to bury this hatchet.

The phone vibrates in my pocket alerting me of my ride showing up. I can't wait for their response and I squeeze both their hands before pushing my way towards the exit. This is not how I wanted this night to end. I take a few steps when I hear Richard's raging voice cut over the noise of the crowd.

"You fucking cunt! I know you're sleeping with her! So what's a little cheating among friends?"

I force myself to keep pushing away from them. The intensity of the dancing kicks up to a fever pitch. I am jostled and thrown around as I struggle. The bumping and grinding turns the dance floor into a mosh pit. I break free and rush out the door, tears threatening to blind me.

I was a fool to think I could have happiness with both of them.

CHAPTER EIGHT

Come With Me Now

The dark scenery we pass on the highway echoes the drowning loneliness of my heart. I exhausted all options to fix our relationship, only to see it turn to ashes when Gracey assaulted Richard. My stomach cramps with anxiety. Gracey is a sore point with Richard. This is all he needed to demand I stop associating with her. There is no way in hell I won't be friends with Gracey, but I also want Richard to love me.

I shake my head to banish those thoughts as the flashing red and blue lights come into view. The plantation house looks eerie illuminated only by the pulsing lights. Jagged shadows flicker into life and vanish in the next heartbeat. The house looks more like a monster looming in the distance than a run-down building.

"Keep the ride meter running and wait for me?" I pat my cheeks to push away the hint of crying and smile at him.

"Sure thing, Princess."

I slide out of the car and make my way to the group of officers surrounding the trespassers.

The police officer tips his hat as his eyes trail along my body before meeting my gaze. My clubbing outfit does not scream real estate mogul.

"You lost, darlin'?"

"I'm Georgina Belmont. You called me."

"Can I see some ID, ma'am?" He shines his Mag-lite into my eyes.

I fish out the ID from the tiny pocket on the skirt of my dress and offer it to him. "Sorry. I was out with friends when you called."

"Mhm hmm," he nods while he looks it over, then hands it back to me. "I'm sorry to call you out here, ma'am. We wanted to make sure there is no damage to the property before hauling away these kids we wrangled up."

"Officer," I make a show of leaning in to read his badge. "Hendricks, I appreciate everything you and your boys did tonight. We both know these kids have been scared enough and have learned their lesson about trespassing."

With that, I lean around him to get a view of the kids on the porch. "Y'all have learned your lesson, right?"

Their heads bob in agreement as they stare up at Officer Hendricks.

"See? Now, please be so kind as to let them all go."

My saccharine smile meets his disgruntled frown. "Looks like it's your lucky night, hooligans."

They scatter like a covey of quail, hopping into their vehicles and high tailing it out of here.

"Officer Hendricks, I appreciate your effort tonight. We're renovating this old place. Even if they have damaged something, it's all going to be gutted."

"You sure ma'am? I don't mind walking through with ya." He glances from me to the house to the man I left playing Clash of Clans in the car.

"Quite sure. I'll lock it back up and be on my way."

"Come on, Hendricks. She said she didn't want to press charges. We let those damn kids go. There's nothin' left here for us. Get her number already and flirt with her on your own time."

Officer Hendricks scowls at his partner and shakes his head. "Fine. Fine. Have a good night, Miss Belmont."

With the flashing lights turned off, it's much darker out here than I realized. I walk back to the car and tap on the window. "You mind waiting another ten more minutes while I check the house?"

"As long as you're paying me, Princess, we're golden." He doesn't even glance up from his game.

I shake my head and wander towards the main house. Without any lights the house is cold and menacing. The massive double doors slide open and I flick on the flashlight on my phone. Sterile blue-white light illuminates a small section of the foyer. Shadows dance as the light plays off the decorations like claws reaching to grab me.

My pulse quickens and the slightest noise causes me to gasp in fear. "Nothing here, Georgie. This place is empty, remember? The cops already cleared it." The words ring hollow as I try to psych myself up.

My heels click on the old floors as I make my way through each room. Nothing obvious is out of place. Drafts of cold air startle me as they brush along my skin. The further from the front door I get, the heavier the air becomes. Despite it being

January in Savannah, beads of sweat break out on my skin.

I creep up the stairs, taking care to keep to the edge in case there are weak spots. The ominous sensation of being watched causes my skin to crawl. Why did I send Officer Hendricks away? I should have called Billy to come walk with me.

I yelp at the first message ding on my phone. My amusement at being spooked by my phone fades when several more messages ding. Richard's chat bubble flashes, drawing my attention to the screen. I shouldn't read the messages until I'm home. I don't want him to think I'm ignoring him. My lower lip hurts with how hard I chew on it in indecision. I tap to bring up the messages.

I can't keep fucking doing this.

I thought you wanted to patch things up, but that wasn't the truth, was it?

There's something different about you now.

This is all Gracey's fault.

I hope you fucking like being her little slut.

You don't deserve my love.

Rooted in place, I blink, dumbfounded at the barrage of messages. What did he mean that I was different? None of this was Gracey's fault. Anger, fear, and pain lash my soul, paralyzing me.

The phone slips out of my hand and clatters to the floor.

The eerie shadows cavort and twist, reveling in my suffering.

All I ever wanted was to be loved by anyone. Richard is my everything. He makes me laugh. He makes me cry. We had the perfect life together, and it's ruined. Richard's cruel words stab into my chest, rip out my bleeding heart and leaving me hollow and forsaken in the dark.

I slump to my knees and my arms wrap around myself. I rock

in place, mourning the loss of the only man I have ever loved and perishing under the guilt of considering abandoning Gracey for him.

Tingles dance up my spine, and I whip my head around to see who's behind me.

A room devoid of even furniture meets my gaze.

I lunge forward for my phone and my body jerks as if my hands have been super-glued to the floor. Muscles strain, and beads of sweat form. I can't lift my hands as I struggle. The harsh wood scrapes my knees and digs into my palms, sending tendrils of pain through my limbs.

I shriek, and jerk my body to free my hands from the floor where I can see they are being held by nothing. The blue light of my phone casts a haunting glow. "Help," I croaked, my voice pinched from fear.

Feathered touches brush along my thighs, teasing between my legs. Warm hot breath fans my earlobe before unseen hands take hold of my hips.

My short, ragged breaths puff clouds into the freezing air.

The feathered touch becomes needier as the sensation mimics Richard's groping hands at the club. My body shivers in anticipation and shame brings the flood of heat to my cheeks.

Desire.

The word purrs in my ear. I want to be desired by Richard, but not here. Not like this. My heart pounds in my chest like I ran all the way from Onga Bongo to here. I thrash and squirm, trying to see who my assailant is, only to find there is no one within touching distance of me. Nothing casts shadows from my phone to suggest a hidden attacker. I am alone in this awful place.

My hand moves of its own volition. The soft sensations between my legs are my own fingers frantically dancing under the sequined dress and panties. I want it to stop. My fingers continue dancing to their own tune. I bite my lower lip and the flames of shame blossom down over my neck and shoulder.

I moan and sob. Every effort to remove my fingers from my throbbing clit only succeeds in me rubbing faster.

I am a dirty slut. I deserve this. I need to be claimed and desired like this.

I twitch and try to jerk my leg free as a caress runs down the back of my thigh.

My shoulders shudder as another runs along my stomach and curls over my breast.

Excitement flares to life as my wetness soaks through my panties.

This can't be happening.

My eyes are fixated on my fingers as my hips grind against them. The invisible touches begin to grow in size and length, beyond fingers and more like tentacles. My nipples grow taut with the pinching suction, and my legs are forced further apart as my fingers rub in furious frustration.

Lightning sensations flash through my body, radiating out and drawing another illicit moan from my lips.

I twitch, trying to thrash against whatever is holding me still. The movements only succeed in more wanton grinding.

Horrified that I'm enjoying this, my eyes widen.

Panting like a bitch in heat, I try to scream for help. Instead, the thick and heavy weight of flesh in my mouth pumps, silencing my screams. The same weighted thickness rubs along my swollen lips, my fingers parting them and allowing the massive member to stretch me.

I whimper and push away from the imagined invading cock, only to have another smooth, heavy tip press along my spread ass.

My skin drips with sweat and I surrender to being held in place on all fours. The only person in the room is me, and the longer these sensations fill every inch of me, the more like tentacles they become. They wrap around my breasts, squeezing them, and kneading them. They pump in and out of me in a rhythmic dance of sin.

White hot ecstasy rips through me as they pierce me over and over without mercy or tenderness. Massive, thrusting pressure pushes deep into my pussy, ass, and mouth. I can taste skin and sweat. The pulsing, throbbing veins rubbing against me short circuit my ability to have rational thought.

Moans of ecstasy spiked with whimpers of pain escape me as a massive cock rips open my ass. Three penetrations are pushing, thrusting, pulling. They swell as my body betrays me and my muscles squeeze tighter, trying to milk them.

Hot salty liquid is pouring down my throat. It is disgusting. Grasping, groping fingers clench and dig into my thighs and breasts while the tentacle cocks pump me full of their juice.

Then they're gone. I collapse to the floor, unsure of what the hell is going on. My breathing is uneven and heavy as I force myself to stay conscious. Regaining control of my arms and legs is like running in water. I grab my phone and shine the light around the room.

I am alone.

The exaggerated sounds of my slow, deep breaths are the only sounds. Once the panic subsides, I start to process what happened. My face burns as the memory of that moment brings both wanton lust to experience it again and abject horror at what I went through.

Why the fuck would I want to do that again? What's wrong

with me?

I cover my mouth and shake my head, trembling in panic. Every lesson a girl is taught on rape is to collect evidence and call the cops. There is no evidence. No semen to put into a rape kit. Nothing in my mouth except my own spit. No blood from losing my virginity. My disheveled clothes are of my own doing and my hand smells of my own sex.

I get to my feet, legs weak from the powerful climax I experienced. The euphoric heaviness of the rush of endorphins, mixed with the horrific shame of enjoying being plowed over and over cause me to stagger as I flee as fast as I can. I have to get out of this place before something else happens.

Thankfully, the Uber driver is waiting for me. I can even see that he is still leaning bored against the door playing on his phone. I fumble with the door handle and slide into the back seat. My voice is rough and shaky.

"615 Forsythe."

"You got it, Princess."

I shiver and hug myself tighter.

This can't be happening.

I use the words like a mantra. What were those sensations? Did I want to fuck Richard deep down to the point I hallucinated a gang rape? It has to be a bad trip. This is nothing like the party drugs Gracey and I had experimented with in Amsterdam. Something horrible happened to me, and the worst part is that no one will believe me.

I start to relax when the house is a memory behind me.

A touch runs down my back and my body stiffens. It's all I can do to not scream in abject terror. I force myself to take a single jagged breath.

"No." I whimper.

The rubbing on my back vanishes in a heartbeat.

"No? Then where do you want to go, Princess?"

"Sorry. Was responding to my phone," I lie terribly.

The driver studies me with concern in the rearview mirror.

"I'm fine. Please. 615 Forsythe."

CHAPTER NINE

Say Hello, Gracey

Every moment is torture as we drive across Savannah back to my apartment. My body aches, and my hands won't stop shaking. I'm on autopilot as I pay the driver and stumble out of his car. I walk into the building and wait outside the elevator, numb to the world. I sway in the hallway, using all my strength to keep from buckling in the hallway. Relieved none of my nosey neighbors are in the elevator, I take a few seconds to close my eyes and make sense of anything that happened at Haven Hill.

The swelling pressure grows at my lips. I scan every inch of the area in front of me, bathed in the light from my phone.

Nothing is there, but the swollen member fills my mouth.

The loud chime of the elevator startles me and my eyes fly open.

I'm safe. It was in my head. Nothing can get me here.

I hurry out. My keys rattle with how hard my hands shake,

making it difficult to unlock my door. Once inside, I turn and lean against the steel door. Unsteady hands turn the deadbolt, latch the chain, and place the chain guard across the plate.

"Nothing happened. It was all in my head," I repeat the words like I'm reciting the Rosary.

The coolness of the door against my flush face gives me the anchor to cling to in this descent into madness. The focus allows me to draw deeper breaths. Too afraid to close my eyes, I fixate on the tiny console table by the door. A tiny photo album flips through the pictures, showing happy memories caught in digital eternity. From beach bums to shopping divas, Gracey and I pose for the camera. On rare occasions, Richard's handsome face pops in behind us.

When I trust myself to move again, I head straight for the bathroom. As I feared, my reflection stares back at me unharmed. Aside from the tear-stain streaks and scrapes on the palms of my hands, there is no hint of being assaulted. I fish out of a washcloth and slide out of my panties. While they are damp from my filthy orgasm, there's no semen or blood to prove three massive dicks tore into my body.

My cheeks flush, and I gasp as my fingers, as if they have a mind of their own, rub along my clit. I shudder and jerk, trying to pull my hand away. The more the memories flash in my mind, the wetter I get.

"No, please, oh God," I beg my reflection.

My fingers stop and I drop to my knees at the toilet. Alcohol burns as it is expunged from my body with what little food I ate this afternoon, and the smell of vomit triggers my gag reflex, making me wretch again.

What's wrong with me?

Another round of dry heaves leaves me shivering and shaking

on the floor of the bathroom. How could I get turned on by rape? I have my fair share of fantasies. Gang rape isn't one of them. I never desire to be abused. I want to be loved and adored. I want sweet, romantic, flower petals clinging to my skin sex..

I'm tripping. Something was in the shots.

The only explanation that makes any sense to me is Richard must have slipped me some kind of I'll-do-anything roofie. The fear of being a sexual deviant fades and breathing comes easier. Lying on the cold tile floor helps me focus and relax.

It's just some weird ass drugs. Ride it out. You'll be okay. You're not a deviant.

With the pep-talk in my head, I push off the floor, brush my teeth and examine the disaster that is Georgina Belmont in the mirror. My hair is limp, my make-up streaks and smudges across my face like a horror movie clown. My dress hits the floor, followed by the scraps of cloth called undergarments and step in my shower.

The water pours icy over my skin for the seconds it takes to eat the water. I crank the dial, and my bathroom fills with a mix of steam as my skin reddens. I scrub until the redness comes as much from the heat of the water as it does my attempts to wash away my sins. Going through the motions of washing my face and hair helps to soothe my frazzled nerves.

The events of the past two days catch up with me and I sob. How could Richard do this to me? How could I be so stupid to believe he wanted to get back together? The rage from yesterday morning blossoms back to life. He lied and connived his way back into my head, again, for what? To get laid?

He only wanted to get laid.

I flinch as the dagger pierces my heart. He never wanted to get married. I pressured him. I forced him to propose with the promises of satisfying his every desire once we were married. The water pours over me, hiding the tears of my revelation. I gave him everything, and he crushed me.

By the time I turn off the shower, my skin is pruned and my tears have dried up, the walls of rage and loneliness forming a cocoon around my shattered heart. We could have worked through the cheating, the anger, and I would have made him the happiest man alive. Then he had to go and drug me. He had to lie and cajole me, then drive me to entertaining giving up my best friend. That ends tonight.

I storm out of the room and grab my phone. If I pause now, I'll cave again. My thumbs fly across the screen as I pound out the words, hitting send without re-reading them.

Don't you ever fucking talk to me again outside of work.

You are lucky I didn't fucking overdose.

Or get hurt at Haven Hill.

I don't know what fucking game you're playing!

It's over.

All I ever did was love you, asshole.

LOVE YOU.

Leave me the fuck alone.

I toss my phone aside and collapse into my massive bed, burying my face into the pillows.

******

The next coherent thought I have is I am going to murder whoever is pounding on my door this early in the morning.

"Go away," I mumble.

Incessant pounding slams against my front door, unperturbed by my command.

"I said go away!" My throat is dry and my voice raspy and when I crack an eye open, I'm blinded by the sunlight flooding into my bedroom.

"Okay, fine! Fuck," I groan as I push off the bed. Every muscle in my body is sore and my head weighs a thousand pounds.

The banging and booming does not relent as I stumble across my apartment. Someone had better have died to be harassing me this early in the morning. I'm surprised Mrs. Feinstein down the hall hasn't intervened.

"I'm comin'. Hold your horses!"

The knocking ceases.. I rest my head against the door as my hand hovers over the locks. I'm in my sanctuary and don't want to burst that safety bubble. What if it's Richard? What if it's my father? I don't think I can deal with either of them this morning.

The door rattles against me as the banging resumes.

I jerk it open and shout, "WHAT?!"

A storm of blue hair and coffee blows by me without even a hello, leaving me to stand dumbfounded in the doorway.

"Were you raised in a barn? Shut the door before you give Mrs. Feinstein an eyeful." Gracey's too chipper for this early in the morning.

I whip my head up at that and see the door at the end of the hall cracked open. I slam the door closed and blush, remembering I'm naked. I mad dash back to my bedroom, covering myself and ignoring Gracey's laughter.

"What are you doing here, Gracey? Shouldn't you be at work?"

"Pretty sure that's my line," she says as she leans in the doorway of my bedroom, crossing her arms and raking her eyes over me before licking her lips.

I freeze, clutching my tank top to my chest. "What do you mean 'your line'? Gracey, can we not today?"

"Georgie, it's two in the afternoon. No one can reach you. Your father took your meeting with the Trinity investors and sent me to check on you." She pushes off the door and her pouty lips draw into a frown as she turns me to face her. Her cool hand against my forehead is wonderful "Everything alright?"

"Yeah. No. Maybe?" I shy away from her fussing over me, shrugging.

"Tell me what happened." Her voice shifts from bemused at my antics to dominating, and she pulls me back to face her again.

Unsure of how to puts words to the madness of last night, I say nothing for several beats. This is Gracey. I can trust her. She'll be proud of me for telling Richard off. I swallow my fear and begin, "Remember how I said the cops called?"

She nods, her grip relaxing on my arms.

"Turns out some teens were partying at Haven Hill and got caught. I started walking the house to make sure they hadn't destroyed anything and..." I let the sentence fade as my thoughts struggle to form into cohesive ideas.

"It felt like I was trippin'. Like one of those drops we took in Amsterdam level tripping." I throw my hands up in frustration.

"It was so much worse, though. I imagined things happening to me and, and I think it's something Richard slipped me." I cover my mouth at my accusation being vocalized. It's one thing to tell Richard off, it's another to tell someone else I think he tried to date rape me.

The soft warmth and tender arms around my shoulders centers me as she pulls me into a gentle hug and I melt into her. All the trauma melts away in her arms. My shoulders relax and I wrap my arms around her waist, clinging to the lifeline that is my best friend. I squeeze my eyes closed and relish the affection.

"What do you need me to do? Tuck you back into bed? Hold you? Take you to the hospital? Fuck your brains out? Kill Dick?"

"Gracey," I protest as I giggle against her. All mirth dries up when I look up.

Her eyes hold a murderous glint and she's staring at me with all the signs of a predator ready to enjoy their mid-afternoon snack. Her nostrils flare, and for the first time since we met, I'm witnessing Sophia Grace raging angry. My spine tingles, like someone walked over my gave when she mentions killing Richard. As if one word from me, Richard would never be seen again.

"No. I don't even know if it was him. I could have eaten something bad. I'm fine. I just needed to sleep. I think I'm going to take the rest of the week off to let things settle down at the office."

Her nose twitches and she huffs.

The deep breath and dramatic motion of drawing her hand down from the top of her head to center herself makes me giggle again.

"Fine. Fine." She gives me one more quick hug. "Seriously, if you need anything, ask, okay?"

"You'll be the first one to know."

I slip from her warm embrace and finish pulling on my pajamas. The frantic shotgun blips of haptic feedback coming from Gracey's general direction cause me to freeze like a deer in headlights.

"What'cha doing?" I ask in a sing-song voice.

"Making that bastard pay. He has no idea how blue his balls are gonna be." Malicious glee paints her pretty face as she stares at her screen.

"Wait… what? Don't send that!" My heart kicks into overdrive as I scurry across the room to take her phone from her before she can hit send, only to discover that Gracey's far more agile than me.

She twists herself from my grapple and hits the send button. "Too late!" She turns the phone like a proud peacock showing their feathers to let me read the message.

"Gracey! Take it back this instant!" I feel the blood drain from my face as I realize she told the entire Gopher pool that Dick slipped me something and it made me sick. "I still have to work with the man!"

"He deserves it." She snatches the phone away from my grasping hands and drops it into a pocket in her dress. "Anyway, even if it is a rumor, he still treated you like shit. Karma's a bitch, and her name is Sophia Grace." She flips her hair as she twirls around and struts her way to my kitchen. "Now, to mend this broken heart of yours."

"Gracey! I mean it. Take it back." I grab her hand to stop her and make her look at me. "I have no idea what happened. We can't ruin Richard's life this way." Bile rises in my throat and my muscles tingle like I'm dancing on a power line. I can't take this.

She steps back up and cups my chin. "Oh, Georgie. You are way too good for that dick. What did you ever seen in him? You're better off without him. I promise. Please let me have this one? Pretty please?" She bats her eyelashes and juts her lip out in a perfect Puss-In-Boots pout.

I cave under her violet gaze. I will always cave to her. "Fine, but the office is going to be unbearable."

She blooms back to life and flounces to the damn cabinet. "It'll be fine. Isaiah will never let him do anything. Enough Dick.

Back to making you feel better." She rummages around. "You always keep an emergency reserve…" She twirls around, triumphant with blueberry muffins in her hands.

I shake my head and remember I have coffee. "Really? Your big plan is to fatten me up with muffins and coffee?"

"Yup! And after…" Oh no, not the big doe eyes. She wants to go shopping. She's smiling and giving me cute, hopeful looks. She'll be relentless if I don't agree to something.

"We go to the mall," I mumble in resignation.

"We go to the mall!" She parrots like a child being told they are going to Disney.

CHAPTER TEN

Love Is a Battlefield

Gracey and I took one glance at my closet, and she forbade me from wearing anything that had Richard's stain on it. This leaves me sporting leggings and a Chelsea sweatshirt. "I can't wear this to work."

"You sure? I bet you'd make the Wolf Pack howl." Gracey says as she wriggles her brows. We both erupt into giggles, and she leads me from the closet. "That's why we're going shopping, silly goose." She boops my nose.

Shopping with Gracey is an Olympic event. Most people go to the mall to wander and socialize, looking at what they don't want to buy. Not Gracey, though. I'm positive there is an entry in the Guinness World Book of Records with her picture for the fastest time to spend ten thousand dollars next to it.

I don't buy my work clothes from the mall. Today I'm letting Gracey be in charge. I've made enough poor decisions this week.

I come to regret this as I stand in a battlefield of discarded clothing in our dressing room. Every piece of clothing imaginable lies on the floor, victim to our two-woman fashion show. I take my time rubbing my hands down the teal knee-length dress. With a set of pearls and matching heels it would be perfect for the Spring. Richard would say it looks amateurish and like every other real estate wannabe in Savannah and would insist on black or navy. I turn to the side and pout at myself in the mirror.

"Ugh, stop thinking about Dick." Gracey pokes me in the shoulder, rolling her eyes. "Well, unless you're thinking about dick. That you can do." She gestures towards her groin wearing a stupid grin.

"Get out of my head. How did you know I was thinking about him?" I turn and motion for her to unzip me.

"When aren't you?"

The soft yellow sundress hanging on the door becomes the most interesting item in the room as I ignore her jab. Yellow is my favorite color. I slip it on and it flares out when I twirl. The second best part of this dress is the pockets.

"Well, shit. Now I can't wear this." Gracey mock grumbles from behind me.

The dress is shimmering and silver, a monstrosity of crystals and sequins meant to mimic mermaid scales, creating a bedazzled vagina effect. The stupid grin on Gracey's face clues me in that she is being sarcastic. "I mean, all you're missing is the word juicy on your ass."

She sticks her tongue out at me, then shrugs, flicking the straps off her shoulders and letting the sparkled mess pool into the corpses of discarded clothing.

Gracey is breathtaking and beautiful. Her blue hair against

her pale skin gives way to the tattoo vines along her arms. They sprawl down her torso to the perfect V of blue hair between her legs. Then curl around her thighs. I've always wondered what her actual hair color is, and why she bothers to dye the hair down there.

She smirks as she catches me ogling her like a teenage boy getting his first glimpse at Playboy. "Like what you see?" she purrs as she prowls toward me.

My heart skips a beat at the sultry smolder in her eyes. Heat blooms on my cheeks and I cover it by turning to inspect myself in the mirror. Blue hair and violet eyes appear over my shoulder in the reflection as her arms curl around me. Contentment washes over me as the tension melts from my body.

"See? All you needed was a hug." Her voice is a whisper against my ear. Her arms wrap around me like the vines around her skin and she nuzzles me.

Her body is warm and inviting pressed against my back. The flush in my cheeks blossoms down my neck and I lean into her, a newfound ache building for her to touch me more. The budding desire is replaced by embarrassment. It's a sin. I pat her hands and pull myself free. "Time to clean all this up," I say, trying to find any excuse to break the tender moment.

Her laugh is melodious and intoxicating as she steps back.

My eyes are drawn down the curve of her hips, sweep of her butt. Her lacy bra struggles to contain her breasts.

"Don't you dare touch any of this." Her voice brings my eyes back up to her face.

Her knowing smirk and hand on her hip, like she's posing for me, means I've been busted a second time.

"We're here to make you feel better."

"I would feel better if you were wearing clothes." I grumble as

I retrieve the fallen soldiers of our clothing battle.

"What?" Her mock indignation gets my eyes rolling, even if I enjoy her antics. "There's nothing indecent showing."

"Uh huh, sure there isn't. Anyway, I'm hungry. Put on something that won't get us thrown out of the food court."

Gracey slips on a dark blue dress that matches mine and we proceed to the counter.

I keep stealing glances her way. Unable to forget the flush of excitement I had in the dressing room. I chalk it up to lingering effects of the drug. She's my best friend. I'm not supposed to want her like this.

"We'll take all of it." Gracey crows in triumph as we reach the cashier.

"Wait. What?"

I pause the woman before she can ring anything up. Gracey flashes me a mischievous grin and a wink as she makes a black card appear out of thin air. I recognize that card. It is the twin to my own.

"Tell me that isn't Richard's."

"Fine. It isn't Richard's."

"Gracey!" I try to grab the card.

She hands it to the lady across the counter and pulls me in close to her. "We're taking all of it."

"No!" I snatch the card back from the clerk. "Gracey. We can't. That's embezzlement and there is no way Richard will let this slide." I point the card at her like a nun with a ruler to smack her hand.

"Okay, unknot your panties." She snatched the card and holds it up to face me. "There, happy?" In silver lettering across the bottom is, Isaiah Belmont.

Mortification and anxiety skyrocket as my eyes

widen. "Gracey, how did you get that card?"

She sulks and huffs. "He gave it to me, dummy. There. Happy. You ruined today." She hands the card back to the clerk.

I droop like a wilted flower to stare at the hem of the dress. "I'm sorry. I-."

"Hey. None of that. I'm teasing you. You have ruined nothing." She nudges me "Your dad said not to tell you because you wouldn't accept it. Since you know, I say we live it up!"

I struggle with the idea of accepting the gift from my father. Is he trying to buy my love? How is it he can talk to Gracey and not me? Gracey's doe eyes and hopeful look whittle away any willpower I was pretending to have. "Okay, fine."

Arm in arm, we lug the heavy bags to the food court. I study her through my lashes as I sip on my milkshake. She is beautiful. I'm not following the inane chatter at all, and she peters out, catching my eyes with hers.

I study my drink to look away from her intense gaze. Has she always glowed like this? Gracey's completely different today, like I'm seeing her for the first time. My chest tightens. I remember these feelings. The pure joy rushing through you when that person is near. Wanting them to focus on you. Wanting them to be with you. This is like the first time I saw Richard.

My breath hitches as the realization strikes me. The hollow pit in my stomach comes back with a vengeance as shame for looking at someone besides Richard slams into me. Before I can dwell on it too much, our snack is done and Gracey is dragging me back out into the mall.

I bowl into her as she stops in front of the next battlefield. "No," I say with all the firmness I can muster.

"Come on, you know you wanna."

"No." I laugh as I balk at entering Victoria's Secret. "I don't need any lacy underwear. I have plenty at home."

She huffs at me. "A girl can never have too many pairs of sexy underwear. Especially stuff she actually likes to wear."

She has me there. All the stuff in my drawers is insufferable to wear. All my choices are things Richard prefers. The last time I went to Victoria's Secret was with him. "Fine! Let's get our sexy on." I roll my shoulders at the absurdity of my battle cry.

"That's my girl!" Gracey leads the charge and we peruse every nook and cranny hunting for our next recruits.

The pink lace peek-a-boo garment fitting my body is soft and pretty. The garters hang loose at my thighs. I could pair it with white stockings and it would be amazing to wear under that teal dress. Richard hates lingerie like this. He prefers reds and blacks with little left to cover the skin.

"This is perfect." Gracey coos as she comes closer. Her smile is soft, and her eyes smolder with desire.

I avert my gaze. My pulse quickens at the idea of Gracey wanting me. "Thanks. Do you really think so?"

"Yup. That color suits you better than Dick's porno choices." She moves away and picks up her next victim.

I fidget with the edge of the lace a heartbeat before taking a sidelong glance at Gracey. She is standing topless in the changing room, trying to decipher a pile of black strings in her hands while also admiring me. Have her vines always curled around her nipples, framing them like small buds? Before she catches me staring, I find anything else in the room to focus on.

"Hey, give me a hand with this contraption, would ya?"

Gracey comes up next to me and forces my attention back to her. We work through the harness, and I hold it in place while she shimmies into it. Her ass is smooth as it curves into my hips while she bends over to work it into place. My pulse quickens as I help her arms through the net.

My fingers trail along her silky smooth skin as I tug the contraption into place. I catch her in the mirror as she cups her breasts to work them into the lingerie she is trying on. I swear she tweaks her nipples while I watch, causing me to tear my eyes away and return to the zipper on the back. Once she's encased, she turns to show me.

My breath catches. The straps crisscross over her body showing and accentuating every last detail. It leaves nothing and everything to the imagination.

"Do you like it?" Her voice is low and husky.

I swallow hard and force my eyes up to hers. Her lower lip is caught between her teeth while she waits for my answer.

"Yeah," I croak, my throat dry. "You're perfect."

Time crawls, measured in heartbeats as our eyes lock. All I can focus on is her. She takes one step forward, tentative, and slow. My heart is in my throat and my lips part as my breathing quickens. She takes another step and the heat of her body as she pulls near is like bathing in the morning sun.

The moment is shattered when there is a knock on the dressing room door. "You two done in there?"

We both flinch back from each other.

"Um, we'll be out in a minute." I call as I turn back to my pile of clothing on the floor.

What is happening here? Am I still high? Am I attracted to Gracey? Does she want me? Have I been blind this entire time? I sneak a glance her way. Her back is to me as she also strips out of the lingerie and is redressing. After giving Richard such hell for stepping out, here I am, looking at someone else.

The sudden rush of confusing emotions and guilt threaten to bring the tears again, and I manage to keep them at bay as we gather up the lingerie we intend to purchase. All the playfulness is sucked out of the air as we purchase the items and retrace our steps to her car. Something changed in the dressing room, and I'm convinced I've made Gracey hate me, too.

I peer out the window as we drive back to my apartment. What is this with Gracey? Will Richard be mad? He always made claims of a relationship between us that I denied. Was Gracey wanting more? Did Richard see what I didn't? Do I want there to be more?

Desire.

I flush with the need for Gracey's affection. The word rattles around my head. Did I think that? I can smell her sitting next to me, sea salt and caramel. It would be easy to reach over and take her hand. It's next to me. I could let her know that we're okay, that I want her to touch me.

I rest my head against the window and close my eyes. What would it be like to have her touch me? My panties grow damp at the thought of her fingers trailing up my thigh. The light drag of her fingernails running up my skin, playing along my tender flesh. I gasp as tingles dance through me from the flick she gives my clit.

"You alright over there?"

The concerned question dumps ice water on the fantasy and my eyes fly open. My clit throbs with need to have her fingers brush over it and a quick glance suggests her hand never moved toward me.

"Yeah. I'm fine." Shame flames my skin from the tips of my ears to my navel, and I hope she's too focused on the road to see me blushing again. I can't tell her that I had a wet dream about her. I would die of embarrassment.

"You sure? You don't look fine."

"It's been a long day. You good if I take a rain check for dinner?"

Gracey looks at me for a hot second before returning her attention to the road. She deflates and moves her hand to put both are on the wheel. "If that's what you want."

"I'm really wiped. I've had a great day, but I don't have it in me for another night out." I want to tell her not to go, that I need to have her fingers inside me. What the hell am I thinking? Why is that what I want? I shift, trying to ignore the dampness of my panties.

"Well, we're here," she says. Her voice is soft.

It rips my heart to shreds to think she's not okay. I should ask her to come up with me. I should talk to her. Tell her all these emotions bouncing around in my heart. But I can't risk it. If I told her and she shot me down, I would be devastated. What if she doesn't feel the same way? Or if she wants more than I can give her? If she were to abandon me too I don't know what I would do to myself.

"Thanks for today. Really. I needed it." I reach over and give her hand a squeeze before getting out of the car. The solemn affair of gathering my bags and walking to the door throws a wet blanket on the amazing day.

At the door, I have the chance to glance back and see Gracey's head against the steering wheel and her shoulders shaking. It wrenches my heart. Fear keeps me from rushing to her. There's something wrong with me. Everything today turned sexual. I don't want these feelings to be because of some stupid drug. Besides, I don't deserve her. I'll ruin everything with her and chase her off like I did Richard.

CHAPTER ELEVEN

What a Girl Wants

Back in my sanctuary, I drop the bags near the door. Once locked, I turn and face the empty apartment. Gracey must hate me now that I've made it weird. What was I thinking going out with her today? Why can't I stop thinking about her? What happens now? She was obviously hurt by me not wanting to go to dinner. Do I text her? Do I leave it alone? Do I call her and tell her I was an idiot and to come back?

I leave the bags where I dropped them as I move to my bedroom. Intending to kick my shoes off and flop face first on the bed. Two steps in and I'm imagining Gracey's pouty lips pressed to mine as she peels me out of my clothes. Her fingers nimble and soft brushing along my stomach to steal between my thighs.

Instead of my bed, I'm staring at myself in the mirror, naked and leaning against the counter as my fingers work my clit into a frenzy. I yelp and jerk back, flinging myself against the wall. I've never been like this. Sure, I have fantasies and desires, but never so needy that I would wet myself at the drop of a pin. My body is thrums in frustration. "Fuck!" I shift, looking for any kind of relief. Maybe I should go to the hospital. They will have some kind of magical mix to flush my system. Then I would have to explain what happened and Richard would get in serious trouble. My father will be furious that I escalated the fight instead of doing what he told us to do.

My eyes settle on the shower and I decide an icy one is in order. I tense, my skin crawls with goosebumps, and I gasp as the chilling water pounds down on my skin. My breathing quickens and I shiver as the water chases away the flames of my sinful fantasies. Relief comes and I switch the water over to hot.

With my eyes closed, I try to focus on anything other than sex.

Gracey's sparkling eyes twinkle to life as she wraps her arms around me. My hands glide over my breasts, imagining they are hers. She gives a faint squeeze, tugging on my nipples to draw them taut. I bite my lower lip, enjoying the faint twinge of pain.

My fingers ease down my flat stomach, following the streams of water until I press into the folds between my thighs. Feathery at first, I trail my finger along the skin until I press the tiny nub. My shoulders curl as I shudder. The sudden rush of brushing touches

Gracey's too mischievous to only tease my folds, so my free hand pinches a nipple while I imagine her teeth drawing it into her mouth. The longer I imagine her touching me this way, the harder my clit throbs under my fingers.

Lost in the fantasy, I lean against the wall and conjure Gracey's lips kissing along my stomach. The light touch of her lips as she pushes my hands away, curling her fingers between mine. I squeeze against her hand as she sucks against my clit. My leg drapes over her shoulder, opening more for her.

Her face burrows deeper between my legs. She nips at my folds before her tongue probes along the edges. My breath is ragged as I float on the edge. I need her inside me. I need more. Yet she teases me, licking and sucking, keeping me primed for release.

My knees lock and my hips shudder as her tongue dives deep inside me. Her nose presses into me, rubbing me as her hands curl around and grip my ass, forcing me to spread wide. My hands curl into her hair and I hold her head tighter to me. Her tongue flicks and digs deep inside me. I press her deeper into myself as I clench and clamp down around her probing tongue.

Her fingers trail further inward, and I gasp as she runs a nail around the rim of my ass.

"Gracey," I whine, "Not there," I plead between panting gasps.

Her finger keeps teasing. I pucker and tighten to keep her out as she continues licking and drinking deep from me. My body rocks in time with her tongue lashes drawing another orgasm from my body. My muscles spasm and pulse. My eyes shoot open as her finger pushes deep into my ass. My hands claw into her scalp, not letting her get away.

She works her finger in time with her lapping tongue. The more she pumps the larger her finger gets, teetering my body between her probing tongue and what is no longer a finger but a throbbing cock.

A second set of hands pushes the water over my skin until my breasts are cupped and squeezed. The pumping grows faster and harder as he pushes me into Gracey's eager mouth. Her tongue laps every drop of me from her. I want this. I want him to fill me and her to taste every drop of my orgasm.

My hips roll back against the invading cock and I cry out as he unloads his seed, rutting a few quick motions before ripping from me.

All sensations are gone. There's no Gracey, no mystery man. I'm alone in the shower, left on my hands and knees with water washing away the proof of my orgasm. No semen, no blood, nothing other than water. I stare at my hand as if I were witnessing a gruesome murder, unable to comprehend how I can feel like I was fucked in the ass, but nothing be there.

I shudder and draw my legs up to my chest, rocking in fear. My eyes stare forward, unseeing as I try to process what just happened. My sexual fantasies are taking on a life of their own. Every sensation and touch was real. My body reacted to it. I'm still aching from the encounter. Gracey's sweet scent is all around me. A thick and heady scent male scent mixes with hers.

What terrifies me most is I liked it, every second.

Beyond tears, I'm left rocking in my shower, trying to will away the needing ache of wanting more. I'm not this kind of girl. I'm a good girl, who does everything they're supposed to. These fantasies are dirty and I'm going to Hell for having them. That should be enough to stop them, but all I want is more.

I shut off the water and dig out a towel to cover myself. As I reach for the hand towel to wipe off the fogged up mirror, movement catches my eye and I whirl around to face my attacker. I knew I wasn't alone. Only, there is nothing there. No man, no Gracey. Pristine white marble tile shines back at me. My heart pounds hard in my chest and my muscles cramp from the fear searing through me.

I'm reminded of those stupid horror tales of "Bloody Mary" where if you say her name in a mirror five times she appears.

Slow deep breath after breath leaves me light-headed as I work to get my nerves under control and turn to face the mirror again.

My reflection is hazy and lacking in detail. Behind me is an obvious blurred outline of a man, a full head taller than me and broad in the shoulders. I squeal in terror as his hand clamps on my shoulder and pushes me forward. My stomach bangs into the edge of the hard countertop as I curl over it. His knee presses between my thighs, forcing them apart.

"No. No! NO!" I shriek as I swing like one of those air weeble-wobbles at car lots behind me, trying to break the grip on my shoulder.

As suddenly as he appeared, he's gone. I scramble back from the vanity and fall flat on my ass, scrambling back like a crab, I stare unblinking up at the mirror.

There is no sign of the man.

I jump up like a jackrabbit and rip open the door to bolt into my bedroom and grab the first thing I can use as a weapon: a stiletto.

My chest heaves from the exertion, and I keep my eyes glued to the bathroom. Like a cheesy cop movie I creep toward the bathroom, ready to fight off my attacker.

I continue this cloak and dagger walk through my apartment, opening every door and turning on every light until I'm convinced there is no one here. Even the front door is still bolted and chained shut. There's no way for anyone to get in and out that way. "The fire escape," I yelp and run back into my room, but the window is locked tight.

I stagger back to my bed and drop the shoe on the floor with the rest of the mess.

Why is this happening to me? All I want is a high school

sweetheart turned husband with two point five kids, a mortgage, and a white picket fence. Not to be someone's wanton sex kitten, bent over every time they feel the urge.

My fingers brush along my stomach and I bite my lip as the idea makes my pulse quicken and the needy ache grows.

No. This is wrong. That's rape. It's not a fantasy.

I flop over onto my stomach and bury my face in my pillow. My clit throbs harder as I squeeze my eyes closed, trying to push the dirty thoughts out of my mind.

Desire

I bite my lip and my fingers slide between me and the bed. The idea of a stranger bending me over and thrusting into me, using me like a whore in a motel makes my clit throb harder. My breath is heavy and labored as my body relaxes in euphoric bliss.

Shame drapes over me like a weighted blanket. I need to tell someone what's happening to me before it gets any worse. But who? It's not like I could ask Gracey to listen to me prattle on about weird, kinky rape fantasies, after today. Richard was my only other confidant, and he is the last person I will ever tell this to. That leaves my father. There is no way I am going to tell my father. He already hates me.

I flop on my back, staring at the ceiling as I rub my hand against my forehead. All my limbs are heavy, like I'm floating in water.

"God, if you're listening, please help me."

CHAPTER TWELVE

The More You Know

January 4, 2019

My alarm bleats like an angry minion and startles me awake. The brightness in the room causes me to believe I've overslept again. My phone says it's only six in the morning. I realize the lights are still on. As I ease out of bed, I retrieve my weapon of choice, just in case the mystery man is the world's greatest hide-n-seek player and is waiting for me in the bathroom.

When nothing terrible happens, I manage to complete my morning routine in record time and get out the door by seven. I won't have to deal with many people if I get to the office early enough and can get back to my life.

I smile like nothing's wrong as I pass the receptionist on the main floor. Gracey's office light is on. The door's closed. I hesitate outside of it, wanting to apologize. After a few seconds, I chicken out and scurry to the elevator. I kick myself for being a coward all the way to the fifth floor.

The lights are off in the main room. I stop at my office first, flicking on the light and dropping off my things before I head to the break room. I'm surprised to see my father standing in front of the coffee machine. He doesn't come in until much later. Why is he here early? I'm not ready to face another round of disappointment this early in the morning.

"Good morning, Georgina. You look lovely today," he says with a warm smile.

I resist the urge to preen at the compliment and reach for my mug before fishing my favorite creamer out of the fridge. "Thanks. It's one of the new dresses."

His piercing gaze never leaves me, and he sips his coffee before he asks, "How are you doing?"

"I'm fine," I reply on instinct. The last thing I want to do is tell him I can't stop having weird rape fantasies after I think Richard roofied me at a night club. He'll either have me committed, or tell me to quit being inappropriate and get back to work.

A scowl forms on his face and he opens his mouth to say something, then closes it, shaking his head. "If you need a day or two to work through your fight with Richard, I'm sure Billy and the boys will be fine."

"I said I'm fine." I grit my teeth and focus on stirring my coffee into my creamer. I don't want to pick a fight with him today. His assumption that I'm the one who needs to take a few days proves more how much he hates me in my mind.

He lingers, studying me before he shakes his head again and grunts out, "Okay, then. Have a good day."

"You too, Daddy," I say as he walks out. With coffee in hand, I retreat to my office.

A few minutes later my desk is littered with colored notebooks, pens, sticky tabs, and anything else I can think of to help me solve my problem. My office supply addiction is one of Gracey's favorite ways to tease me. Today, I'm putting them to good use. I'm too smart for this. I'm going to solve this problem and move on with my life.

I stare at the blank page with faint black lines. What am I going to do? How does someone even begin to uncover why they behave this way? I can't believe any kind of drug slipped into those drinks would last for more than a day. Nothing I found in google searching even comes remotely close to describing what I experienced while tripping.

I tap my pen against my lips with the pen and decide the only way to figure this out is to start by listing all the issues and prioritizing them. My pen makes a furious scratchy noise as I hastily write what issues I have to deal with. The list is short, Haven Hill, money, Richard, Gracey, and sex dreams.

What else do I need?

I close my eyes and the flash of the man in the mirror blazes like a movie screen on my eyelids. I gasp and open my eyes, adding 'mystery man' to my list.

A colorful grid appears on the page to divide the experiment up. The scientific method was going to save me.. All of the details I can think of are written in swirling font, each owning a color of the rainbow. Each getting a column for theory, test, and results until I'm satisfied I can track and record every detail of what's happening to me.

A small knock on the door breaks my focus.

"Georgie?" Gracey hovers in the entry with a small ream of paper in her hands.

"What's up?" I get up and come around the desk.

"I need you to fill out the billable hours for your crew." She fidgets with the edge of the papers, ruffling them under a finger. She won't make eye contact with me.

We both freeze when my fingers brush along hers as I reach to take the papers.

She pulls back, leaving them with me, and doesn't stay to talk like every other morning.

I watch her retreating form, trying to not feel the sting of rejection. The papers crinkle as my grip tightens.

I am done with the pile by the time lunch comes around.

My routine continues being thrown off kilter as Gracey and Richard aren't at my door to cajole me into lunch shenanigans. The weight of being abandoned is too much and I gather the finished papers, my journal, and purse to start my lonely new lunch life. I stop again outside Gracey's door. The office is dark this time. I drop the papers into her mailbox and head to the restaurant across the street.

In a booth in the back of the restaurant, I study my journal, unsure of which item on my list to tackle first. A small deli sandwich sits untouched before me next to a large, sweet tea in a plastic cup.

My eyes keep drifting to 'mystery man' and 'mirrors'. There was a man in the mirror and I'm not crazy. How do I prove it? The restaurant is hopping with people on their lunch break. I can't very well go into the bathroom and perform a seance at the mirror. Drumming my fingers on the table it dawns on me that I have a mirror with me.

My hands tremble as I retrieve the compact from my purse. Holding it between both hands, like the man might jump out of it, I ease it open. My scrunched-up face is all I see in the tiny circle, so I set the compact on the table. I pick up my pen and scribble a few notes about him not appearing out of thin air.

The minutes tick by as I stare at the compact, unsure if I'm trying to summon him, or grateful he's not there. Then it dawns on me. The mirror was fogged up in my bathroom. A quick huff and puff over the mirror and try again.

I stare, transfixed at the blurry outline hovering over my shoulder. Cold sweat runs down my back as I try, and fail, not to shake. I lower my arms and watch in fascination as the mirror clears up and the image fades. Breathing heavy, I snatch up the mirror and huff onto it a second time.

While the reflection is blurred with the fog, the outline is present.

The third time the figure is clearer, and he smiles at me. I yelp and slam the compact closed. The people around me turn and look. When nothing happens, they resume their lunch.

I jot down what I saw and how I got the man to appear. My chest hurts and my stomach's too knotted to bother with eating lunch. I wasn't expecting anything to happen. What am I supposed to do with this information? Should I get a priest? Is this a demon? After a moment's pause, I write those questions down too. I needed to know if I was manifesting this. I look over my shoulder to verify there is no one there and no one can get behind me.

I ease open the compact and blow hot air against the mirror.

The figure forms and waves at me.

Frozen in place, I stare long after the fog clears. My brain short-circuits trying to rationalize what's happening. When I pull myself from the mirror, I return it to my purse.

January 4 12:34 PM

Male figure appears over my right shoulder when the mirror is fogged. It waved at me. Nothing sexual happened. Am I possessed? Or am I hallucinating due to a nervous breakdown?

Next Steps:

Try again at home.

Record with camera for proof.

Wave back???

~~See if other people can see it.~~

If I'm the only one who can see it, and I try to have them see it, what will happen to me? Not willing to risk being locked away forever, I decide to keep this to myself until I have more to go on.

My lunch abandoned, I head back to the office. I have to get the budget put together for Haven Hill and the last thing I need is a mental breakdown because my love life is falling apart. I crank my Spotify and leave the door closed as I plug the numbers into the spreadsheet. Normalcy helps to ease my frazzled nerves, but my focus only lasts a few hours.

I race out the door by five and wind up in Best Buy where I spend more money than I should on anything I think might help me record what's happening to me. The Uber driver gets an extra tip for helping me carry my assortment of bags to the building door.

My apartment is a disaster and is in no state for a controlled experiment. First on the list of tasks is to clean up. I deposit the bags on my kitchen island and change into comfy clothes. I run my fingers through my hair and survey the hurricane level disaster Gracey and I left from the center of my room. "Okay. Pick one thing and start, Georgie."

I start with laundry. Gathering up dirty clothes and tossing them into the hamper. Then I focus on picking up trash and taking it all to the chute down the hall. Then it's on to dishes, followed by wiping everything down with wipes, and finishing with vacuuming. By the time I finish, it's late.

My muscles are sore and I'm tired from the long day. With everything organized, put away, and my apartment shining like the top of the Chrysler building, I relax. I can pretend I'm in control of my life again and put this horrible week in the rearview mirror.

CHAPTER THIRTEEN

Knowing is Half the Battle

The sweet siren call of hiding under my covers and drowning my sorrows in Cherry Garcia is tempting. Proud of myself for resisting, I grab the small army of office supplies I brought home and crack open my experiment journal.

Mr. Mirror exists only when the mirror fogs. The question remains if I'm hallucinating him, or something worse. I scribble all the worst plausible options like I'm making a grocery list. The last courtesy of the history segment on Ghastly Renovations running in the background.

Schizophrenia

Multiple personality disorder

Nervous breakdown

Brain tumor

Possession.

The last time I used the scientific method, I was a teenager, so I spend a few minutes on Google reminding myself of what it entails. There can be no mistakes and I can't fix whatever this is if I'm sloppy.

Experiment Two - Mr. Mirror
Question: Is it possible to communicate with Mr. Mirror?
Research: I proved he will appear in the mirror when it's fogged up.
Hypothesis: I can summon Mr. Mirror every time I create mirror fog.
Hypothesis Two: I can communicate with him.
Experiment: I will set up one camera in the bathroom. Fog the mirrors by running the shower as hot as possible and wait.

My journal abandoned on the couch, I spring up and dig through the bags until I find the tiny video recorder and tripod. The people who package video equipment are sadists and owe me a butter knife. Ten minutes of my life are gone before I manage to free them from their boxes.

Fear stills me as I stand in the doorway to my bathroom. When I was cleaning, I was too distracted to think about Mr. Mirror. Entering with the purpose to summon him and capture him on camera causes my feet to become cemented in concrete. My fingers tighten around the gear and my breathing kicks into overdrive.

"You got this. You just need to catch him. Then you can run out of the bathroom."

I force one foot forward, then another, and once in, I'm able to function again. I set the tripod on the floor and get the camera attached. It dawns on me that the camera may be dead. "Shit," I mutter and check if I can plug it in. Happy that it records while plugged in I make a tiny intro video.

"Experiment One. Well, Two. One was the restaurant, but I didn't.. Nevermind. Experiment Two. I'm Georgina Belmont. It's Friday, January 4, 2019, at about…well it's not important what time it is. It's late. If everything goes well, we'll see Mr. Mirror and prove I'm not crazy. Bye!" I wave at the camera, then press the button on the tiny remote to stop recording.

"Ugh.. This isn't a TikTok, Georgie."

I rub my hand over my face and roll my eyes at myself. I crank the water to the hottest setting my shower allows and step back to close the bathroom door. As much as I want to keep it open, I don't want the lack of steam to be a reason the experiment fails. I check the handle three times to make sure it's not jammed before I move to my sink.

The last time he formed, he tried to bend me over the counter. Will he only appear if I'm aroused? I hope not. I shudder and my skin crawls at the idea. My body won't stand still as I wait for the shower to create a sauna in my bathroom. As the mirror fogs, I check the camera and frown. A quick scan of the room for a solution and I snatch my hand towel to wipe the lens of the camera and re-check the screen.

The mirror streaks into the patterns from my impatience of wiping it with a towel when I'm getting ready. Like a Disney movie's magic, my reflection is shadowed by a male figure. He's a few inches taller than me. As he forms, warmth grows behind me, but he does not touch me.

I stand firm, staring at the blurry man behind me, despite wanting to snatch my camera and run for the hills. I try to make out any real details I can. The longer I stare the more details I can make out. Tousled dark hair, a blue jacket that reminds me of a uniform.

"Can you hear me?" I whisper.

He nods and I let out the breath I had been holding. The rational part of my brain tells me I'm alone in the room and this is my brain telling me what I want to hear. My eyes see a different person responding to me.

"Do you intend to kill me?"

The shake of his head brings an equal amount of relief. At least my mind is not trying to murder me.

"Why did you rape me?" I cross my arms and huff.

His hands move in frustration. His mouth moves like he's talking. The only sound is the hiss of my shower water.

"No? You didn't rape me?" My shrill question is one step under a shriek as my temper flares to life.

He holds his hands in front of him, like he's placating a wild animal and shakes his head again.

I'm even more confused by his lack of communication. I need to know the answer to this. What's happening to me requires some kind of explanation, even if it is my mind rebelling against my body.

He studies me through the reflection before he hangs his head in shame before he nods.

My chest tightens and heaves as I try to catch my breath. I don't know what I expected to happen, or do, with the confirmation. The maelstrom of emotions is preventing me from thinking rationally. Vengeful anger ruins any further communication as I storm to the shower and turn it off, followed by yanking the door open and turning on the vent fan. My hand swipes across the fog in a frantic and violent manner to erase Mr. Mirror from my life. I will never take a hot shower again.

"Et tu Brute?" I accuse my reflection of betraying me. Why do I hate myself so much? Why don't I deserve happiness?

I wish my reflection would give me all the answers. She remains silent. My only comfort is I recorded everything. I grab the camera off the tripod and leave the bathroom behind to return to my lab, the couch.

Tears roll down my cheeks as the mysterious wavy-haired man is nowhere to be seen. The camera only recorded me talking to myself in the mirror. With the failure of the experiment I stare at the page I wrote on, wiping away the tears on my sleeve.

Data Analysis: Nothing to see. The camera did not record anything. I know what I saw. He answered me. He raped me.

I'm left shaking at my written confession. Can I say it's a he if it's my mind? Is it rape if it's self-inflicted? With a trembling hand, I continue.

Conclusion: I can summon him when the mirror fogs and I can communicate with him.

Communication: I don't ever want to talk to him again.

I slam the book closed and toss it away. I've had enough of this crap for tonight. I thought I was clever trying to perform a science experiment for madness. At least I can bury my woes in Cherry Garcia and Moscato wine.

I flip through the channels and end up on reruns of Ghastly Renovations, my favorite renovations show. Even that comfort fails me as all I focus on is his apologetic gaze followed by the helpless rage boiling to the surface from his confession. Why would I do this to myself? Was this punishment for denying Richard and losing him?

I curl into myself on the couch, the Cherry Garcia untouched on the coffee table. Maybe Richard had seen this side of me and that's why he cheated. He doesn't want a broken wife. No one will. Not even Gracey can stand to look at me anymore. The way she acted today, she must have seen it, too. It's obvious. I don't deserve happiness. Even my mind knows I'm only good for being used and abused then discarded.

"Trouble in love?" The commercial's narrator filters through. "Feel like you're all alone with no one to turn to?"

I crack one tear rimmed eye open and watch stock footage of depressed people slumping around the house.

"Fear not. I can help you turn your life around with just one call!" A young black woman with purple contacts points at the screen. "Call 1-800-PSY-CHIK today. You are not alone." Large block letters write out the telephone number on the screen.

I roll my eyes and curl back into myself. I don't need a fake psychic to tell me I'm done for. At least with my phantom rapist I can imagine that I feel good.

"Don't hesitate, call now! That means you Georgie."

I jolt back to attention and watch the screen. The commercial is over and the show comes back on. I scramble for the remote and push the back button. Thanks to the magic of DVR I watch the woman pointing at the screen in reverse and hit play. What did she say?

"Don't hesitate, call now! That means you, Georgia!"

It's confirmed. I'm losing my mind. I think commercials are talking to me. I turn my back to the TV and bury myself into the couch.

CHAPTER FOURTEEN

Pest Control

My dreams are tormented by shadowy men chasing me. Holding me. Tearing at my clothes. Monstrous cocks flaring to life and ejaculating acidic poison at me. I fight and struggle, scrambling away only to be caught again.

I wake up, my heart hammering, drenched in cold sweat. The TV drones on in the background. Every muscle in my body is sore and aches. I push myself off the couch and stretch. I stumble into the kitchen and take a swig of milk from the jug. I don't know how much more of this bullshit I can take. My phone blares an alarm from the bedroom.

"Fuck. I did agree to that, didn't I?"

People assume that a realtor's job was some cushy nine-to-five Monday through Friday or a bunch of free time sprinkled with random house showings. It is both and more. Today is Saturday. I agreed to go to a foreclosure with Billy to assess if it was worth renovating. I shudder and whimper under the cold shower. I have to be presentable and I refuse to allow my rapist another crack at me.

The travel mug is warm and soothing in my hands as I wait at the door to my apartment building for Billy. The sun is still wrestling itself out of its cradle and the skies are a mix of grays and pinks. The rumble of Billy's truck can be heard from blocks away. There was a time I would be up at dawn every morning enjoying morning exercise before rushing off with Billy and crew to breathe life back into unloved houses. Today is not one of those days. All I want to do is crawl into bed and hide from the world.

I put on a brave face as I push through the door and hop up into Billy's truck. Maybe Dad's right, and I need to hide away all my bullshit. If no one finds out I'm broken, then I can slip by without having to worry them.

"Mornin', Miss G."

"Morning, Billy," I say. The fake chipper tone draws the side eye from Billy as he puts the truck into drive.

He takes his time getting to the walk-up, singing with his country music, and leaving me to my own thoughts. My mood improves as we pull to the curb in front of the place. There's a brick wall running along the sidewalk grown over with vines. A small wrought-iron gate is set at the end of the walk up to the building.

"Isn't that cute," I say, leaning forward to look at the house through the windshield.

A genuine smile settles on my lips. The joy in taking a house on the verge of becoming a pile of rubble and turning it into someone's dream home is my love language. Four years in school for an architecture degree let me flash that fancy degree under my Dad's nose to get this part of the workload. I breathe in the damp morning air. Musty wood and fresh soil greet my nose.

"Looks like a tetanus shot waiting to happen."

"Billy! Where's your sense of creativity? Let's hope the bones are still good." I eye the partially collapsed roof on the edge of the porch and let Billy lead after taking the flashlight he hands me.

His footsteps tell me the porch has at least a few solid boards left in it. He taps at the lock box and pops out the key to let us in. The lights flicker to life. He grins at me when nothing trips the breaker.

Most of the first floor is covered in debris and dust. Tags mark the walls showing that local kids have partied here more than once. The stench of death slams me in the face. There must be a bunch of dead rodents rotting away. This kind of thing is common in abandoned properties. It never gets easier to smell. I cough and cover my nose as my eyes tear up.

"Miss G, if you want to wait here I can finish the inspection and let you know." Billy stands in the doorway, denying me entry. Billy never refuses me walking a house with him.

"Nonsense. I'll be fine. Now, let's look at this place!"

He hesitates. Before I can insist, he relents and lets me pass through the doorway.

Soft spots in the floor cause us to step with caution, but the walls appear to be solid. The two of us share our ideas for the space and what options we have available to us. The upstairs is the same, except one bedroom sports a collapsed portion of ceiling. That will be trouble.

"Think it's worth getting?" Billy asks as he offers a hand for me to steady myself on the last few steps.

"Depends on the price. I wonder how bad the electrical and HVAC are." I'm not looking at Billy as I stare at the ominous door to the basement. Where everything else is old and run-down this door is in pristine order. No blemishes, or tags, clean on the hinges and closed. My curiosity burns, making my fingers tingle. I need to know what's behind the door.

"We both know they'll both need to be replaced. We can build the costs into the budget. No need to go look at 'em."

In all my time working with him, he always wants to inspect something with his own eyes before making an estimate. Why is he being weird today? "It won't take that long. Let's get it checked out and then we're out of here, okay?"

I don't wait for a response and try the door. It opens into the stairwell, so we'll have to fix that. I creep down the rickety basement stairs. The pool of light from my flashlight shows an unfinished root cellar. My nose crinkles at the sight of a muddy floor, glad I'm wearing tennis shoes for this walk through.

The stairs creak and groan under the weight of Billy as he follows me down.

Shining the light on the joists, they appear to be in good order and don't give when I push on them. We'll have to do something regarding the height. If they're low enough I can reach them, they're too low for someone like Billy. Following the piping to the utilities, the old furnace sits long forgotten in a corner atop a slab of stone.

"Going to have to do something about that." I mutter and continue sweeping my light looking for the breaker panel.

"Oh?" My light stops in its tracks as I highlight a heavy steel door with a massive brace lock set into the foundation. "Is that a wine cellar or a vault?"

"Not sure, Miss G. Whatever it is, it's rusted up tight.

Especially down in a place like this. We'll get it open and find out what's in there with the full crew here." Billy's hand rests on my shoulder to stop me.

I flinch and try to recover it by waving my hand at him. "Nonsense! We're here, we can at least try the door."

The latch for the door retracts without resistance.

"See?" I chirp as I swing it open. "Nothing to worry about."

CHAPTER FIFTEEN

Who Do You Think You Are?

The dank, musty scent of mold and mildew slams me in the face as I open the steel door. My light flickers into the opening and illuminates racks along the walls of a stone-lined wine cellar.

"Oh!" I squeal with delight. "I wonder if this was a bootlegger's stash with that kind of security."

I have no idea if this house is even that old. If we find prohibition era alcohol it will pay for the top tier finishes. I step onto the paving stone walkway and examine the dusty bottles. They are all full and unlabeled, making them worthless.

Movement down the hall catches my eye. I jerk the light to find more wooden racks. Skittering on the stone tells me we are not alone.

"Billy? I think we have a friend." My light keeps scanning, looking for the rodent. "It's alright, I won't hurt you," I coo to the darkness. The last thing I need is a panicked squirrel flinging itself in my face.

A hint of a reflection at the edge of my light gets me to twist and look that way.

"Dang this little guy is fast." I step deeper in, trying to figure out how it got into this place.

Golden eyes flare to life under my light deep in the far corner. They are much too high to be a rat or squirrel. I should be afraid. It's either an enormous rat, or a monster. Where's Billy? Why am I not running? A sense of calm washes over me and I lower my light, my fingers going lax and allowing it to clatter to the floor.

The eyes remain as bright as shining the light on them, and hold my gaze, searing into my soul.

My mind numbs and I take a stumbling step forward.

The eyes beckon me forward.

My only thought is the need to get closer. My body jerks. My feet won't move.

The eyes call to me.

I try to lean forward and my body trembles as if my brain is rebelling against my wishes. I need to get to those eyes. Instead, I take a step back. Adrenaline spikes through me and my body jerks as I try to force myself forward, only to take another step back. Like a puppet on a string my limbs move in an awkward and herky-jerky fashion away from the eyes that need me to come to them.

A dark hiss echoes from the corner.

Light blinds me and pain radiates through my chest as if I have been put in a vice grip.

"Miss G? Everything alright?" Billy's deep voice is laced with concern. It has a growl I've never heard before.

I can move again and I'm afraid. Where did my flashlight go? Why does everything hurt?

Billy stands next to me, his light scanning the space around us.

We are alone.

I shake my head, still trying to piece together what happened. A shiver rips down my body.

"Let's get you out of here. We'll have the boys take care of the pests. We'll explore the house proper when buy it, okay?" He wraps his arm around my waist and leaves no room for arguments as he guides me out of the wine cellar and out of the basement.

"Okay." I give him no resistance, using his brute strength to steady myself. My heart hammers in my chest, making it hard to draw breath.

He keeps his arm around me as we make our way back into the root cellar. Then he doesn't release me while he slams the door shut.

When he doesn't let me go after, I swat at his hand.

"Billy Coeh! What would your wife think of you manhandling me like this?" I make no movement to escape his clutches.

"She would want to know if she could join in, all things considered." He gives me a rueful grin and winks.

My cheeks flare to life with blushing heat. Thoughts of running my fingers along his rippled chest dance through my mind. Hands rest on my hip that aren't Billy's and hardening manhood brushes against my ass. I squirm out of his arms and stumble back.

No!

Nothing more happens. I turn and hurry back up the stairs and out the door, gulping down the fresh air once on the porch. I can't even deal with the idea of being attracted to Billy Coeh. I'm gearing up to give Mr. Mirror holy hell for messing with me while working.

"Miss G? I'm sorry." Billy calls as he follows behind me.

I wave my hand and shake my head. "Not you. The smell got to me." I pull my phone out of my pocket and call the bank. "Good morning, Janine."

"Good morning, Miss Belmont. What can I do for you today?"

"I'm interested in the place on Holly Way."

"Oh good. It will be going to the auction block this afternoon along with three other properties."

"Well… what would say to closing it early and not sending it to auction?" I pace, like a long-tailed cat in a room full of rocking chairs.

"I'm sorry Miss Belmont. It's policy to send it to auction."

"Yeah, and we both know this place isn't going to get the fifty-five you're asking for it. The land itself is only worth thirty. Then you throw in the reno work and no one is going to touch it with a ten-foot pole at that price."

"What are you offering?"

I knew she would bite. A place like this would cost them more money in auction fees than taking my offer. I'm the only one who knows about that wine cellar.

"I'll give you thirty-five. It's the best offer you're going to get."

"Miss Belmont, be serious. We both know that is highway robbery for that property. The lowest we can accept is fifty-five."

I wink at Billy. "What about forty and I throw in a word with my dad?"

The line is silent for a full minute. "Dinner."

"Deal."

"Then, Miss Belmont, you better get here before lunch to complete the paperwork."

I hang up and grin at Billy.

"You know your father is going to kill you when he finds out."

"Stop being a worrywart, Billy. It'll be fine."

He laughs and shakes his head before we load back into his truck and he takes me home. The entire ride home, the teakettle of my temper simmers to a boil. The only explanation for what happened in that wine cellar is he forced my body to move backwards. First he rapes me, now he's taking over my body.

"See you, Monday," I chirp to Billy and hurry back into my apartment. I know I said I never wanted to talk to him again. This is unacceptable and I will not tolerate it.

I approach my bathroom like I would a scared animal, afraid of what may happen. I can't believe I'm going to do this. This may be the worst idea I've had to date. I stand before the mirror, keeping my rage in check while the steam builds. When it gets to the point where my hallucination appears I point at it in the mirror like an angry school marm.

"Did you fucking stop my legs from working?"

It nods. I jerk to turn off the water and run away. My entire body is not responding. My muscles shake as I try to get them to respond to me. My ears ring. That first night in the mansion flashes back. My arm raises and moves on its own.

"No. No, no no. Stop. Please," I plead.

My arm continues to move to the mirror, followed by my finger tracing along the glass.

TALK

My mind races in circles. It wants to talk. My own fucking mind wants to talk to me. It took over my fucking body. I should get help. Find some kind of head shrinker that can pump me full of medicine to make this go away. If it can control my hand, it can write. My breathing is rapid and shallow. I continue to stare unblinking, my eyes starting to hurt.

"Don't ever do that again."

The man in the mirror nods.

"Fine. We can talk."

He nods again, and I shut off the water. I sit at the kitchen table with a notepad in front of me and a pen.

"How does this work?"

My right arm twitches. I flex it and it twitches again. Is he asking permission to use it?

"Do it already!" I snap at my hand.

It lifts the pen and starts writing in flowing cursive.

Hello. It is a pleasure to meet you.

I stare in disbelief as I am left-handed. I tried once to write with my right hand; it looked like a toddler's scrawl. This penmanship is even finer than my flowery cursive.

"What do you want from me?"

I only wish to bring you comfort. I am sorry for what has happened to you. I never meant for it to go as far as it did.

"What the fuck does that mean? 'Meant for it'?"

My hand pauses as if it is lost in thought.

I can't explain it. When you are filled with longing, my need to satisfy you becomes overwhelming. Again. I am sorry.

I think back to all the times I was taken by my imagination. Maybe he was telling the truth, and he never meant to hurt me? What if it was uncontrollable for him. Wait, am I justifying him raping me? Oh, hell no.

"You still fucking raped me. Why should I believe anything you have to say?"

Yes, I did rape you. I am not trying to excuse my actions. I am trying to give you understanding as to the circumstances we find ourselves in. I am as much a slave as you are to your desire.

I want to argue and rage at him that there is no excuse for his behavior. That regardless of how he tries to rationalize it there is no forgiveness. He admits it was rape. My vindication is short-lived. My eyes stare at that last word. A dark echo rattles through my skull.

Desire.

The voice is feminine, and very much not mine or his. Shivers flow up my spine as it speaks. Heat radiates through my body and I breathe harder. My vision swims as I need to touch myself become overwhelming.

"No... no... no..." I beg.

The urge does not relent.

Then arms wrap around me. I am being held against his chest. Comforting warmth rages against burning heat. I rock in the chair as I try to move my arms to finger myself. I need to satisfy myself, but my hands stay curled up to my chest, pinned by his muscular arms. Tears stream down my cheeks as my heart hammers in my chest.

Time crawls as I agonize. I want sweet release. I focus on the arms, needing his strength to stop me. The wave recedes and I draw my first full breath. My body shakes as I lay against the table. What the fuck was that? I struggle to get my thoughts in order.

"What... what was that?" I whisper.

My right arm glides over to the paper.

That was your desire. I try to protect you as best I can. As soon as you give in I am drawn to you like a moth to the flame. Your need fuels my need. Just as you struggle to resist, so do I. Once we are lost to passion, it must play out. I humbly beg of you your forgiveness. I know it is not something easily given. But Georgina, I truly never wanted any of this for you.

I don't care if he's lying or manipulating me, that other voice terrifies me, and his arms around me bring a sense of safety to me.

"I… can't forgive you. What you have done is… No." I shake my head and set down the pen. I can't read any more of his excuses. I can't let him try to sweet talk his way out of this.

"Just… leave me alone."

He nods, his chin pressing against my head as he cradles me, and then he is gone. I sit alone. Longing aches between my legs. Tears hang heavy in my eyes. Worst of all, a dull void aches where my heart once was.

I am truly alone.

CHAPTER SIXTEEN

My Name is No

The notepad with the sprawling handwriting taunts me every time I walk past the table. My muscles tense and there is a pause, where I consider caving and continuing the conversation. Then I remember everything that's happened grow angry, refusing to succumb to this madness.

I lean against my kitchen island staring at the notepad as I sip my coffee.

Don't do it, Georgie. You need professional help. Maybe you should get dressed and go to church instead of passing notes with yourself.

I know better. My curiosity will gnaw at me like a dog with a bone. I have to know more, to see what my mind has in store for me. Maybe if I let this ride out, it will go away and I can move on with my life. Squaring my shoulders I march over to the table and plop into the chair. I pick up the pen in my right hand.

"Okay, Mr. Mirror, are you there?"

Yes.

I suppress the urge to drop the pen and flee. Even with the knowledge of asking if he's there, it's terrifying to think another entity is hovering around me.

"Who are you?"

Nathaniel Horn, Sergeant, Army of the Tennessee, XV Corps. Born 1842, Pittsburgh, Pennsylvania. Deceased December 7, 1864, Savannah Georgia.

"You were in the Civil War?"

I was a scout and accompanied General Sherman in the March to the Sea.

"How did you die?"

I, the hand pauses and taps the pen against the paper, *don't remember. There are vague impressions. Nothing concrete I can tell you. I'm sorry.*

Yup, all in my head. My brain decided I needed a young strapping soldier from the Civil War to bend me over a counter.

"Is there anything you can tell me?"

I remember the house. I remember being lured in by the offer of a warm bed and hot food. Then it is all a jumble.

I let out an exasperated huff. "Fine. Do you remember anything after that?"

* * *

Bits and pieces. Most of the time I am, again he pauses to think, not asleep, but not aware either. That is until he anguish and loneliness compels me to act. Like with you. It pulls me towards you. I have to comfort the source of those emotions. I remember all of them as if they're here with me. The in-between is a blank oblivion.

"Wait… What? What do you mean *them*?

Yes. My brides, like you.

"I'm not your bride. I'm no one's bride. I'm not even dating anyone! What in the hell do you mean, bride?"

We are one body. My soul and yours are entwined. It is the only thing that makes sense.

Icy terror seeps into my bones, causing me to shiver. "No. How do we undo this? I never asked for this. I don't want to be your bride."

You cannot. You and I are one. I will be with you forever, as a husband should be.

"We are not husband and wife!" I scream at the pen as if it is Nathaniel. "What are you? How did you get in my head? Why are you torturing me?"

At Haven Hill, your despair and grief called to me. I wanted to protect you from the pain and suffering you were experiencing.

That was when I joine-

The pen clatters against the far wall. Sweat trickles down my back and goosebumps run along my arms. I struggle to draw in a full breath as I clutch at my chest. The quiet is shattered by the roar of my pulse in my ears and my vision swims.

He did all of this to me. How messed up am I that I would do this to myself? It has to all be in my head. There's no way the spirit of a dead Civil War soldier was raping me. Ghosts are not real. Darkness creeps in around the edges of the world. All I can see is the wood of the tabletop. This was all my doing.

All thought leaves my head as the palm strikes across my face. Bright flashes of light dance as my body draws in a much needed full breath. Blinking, I reach up to check my cheek. My probing touch does not bring any further pain. The original pain was already fading like a creepy nightmare.

"Was that you?" The screech echoes through the empty apartment.

I huff and stomp over to the damn pen and flop back into the chair and slam the ballpoint tip onto the paper, leaving an ugly smear. "Explain yourself."

Yes. The slap was me. You were going to pass out if I didn't get your attention. Just like after I am asleep, my joining with you is hazy. The first clear memory I have is when you told me to stop in the car. I am sorry if I hurt you in the house. I don't have any recollection of those moments.

"How convenient." I stifle the urge to throw the pen again. "Fine. How does this work?"

* * *

I will try to be as unobtrusive as I can. As long as your desire does not claim you, I will not touch you. Once you are drawn in, I will be forced to follow along.

"And do what? What is it you do when I lose myself to this desire bullshit?"

I can give you any experience. Everything you desire. Every touch. Every scent. Every taste. It is my duty to give you everything.

"That makes little sense. Stop talking, writing, whatever in riddles. I need answers!"

In response, a hand slides on top of mine, gripping the pen over the top of my hand. He leans over me, reaching over my shoulder to hold the pen with me. Hot breath runs along my ear, teasing and intimate. Warmth from his body floods along the right side of my back where he presses against me. As quick as it appears, it vanishes.

That is what I mean.

"Does that mean you're standing behind me?"

No. We are one body, one soul. I trick your mind into feeling me standing behind you. I've learned my br-, the pen scratches out the word he started to write, *hosts respond better to external stimuli.*

"So you're a magic man-spirit thing that rapes women and then tags along for the ride after?"

* * *

Your words are harsh. I have no ill intentions toward you. My soul is your soul. I prefer to think of myself as a free spirit that tries to bring comfort to lonely souls.

"You are not comforting."

My eyes slide closed in thought as I rub my temples. The sense of overwhelming sadness mixes with my burning rage. How can I be sad and angry about not comforting myself at the same time? What did I expect from my own hand? Spirit? Man-thing? My eyes fly open as I stare at my hand.

"Prove to me you're not me." However this plays out, I'm ready to be amazed by my madness.

My mother is Anabelle Horn, a seamstress. My father is Jacob Horn, a farrier. You should be able to use your goo-goo thing to find them.

Why didn't I think of that? I drop the pen on the paper and pull up my laptop. Google searching leads to Ancestry where I begin the morbid task of creating a family tree linked to me, hoping to get hits on the information 'Nathaniel' provides me.

I pay for the access, refusing to be thwarted in this quest. It's not a waste of money if it proves I'm not crazy. Result after result comes back with the data I have from the notepad, until I am staring at census records of Jacob and Annabelle Horn, as Nathaniel said. Then, staring at me is a lone picture of a young man in a Union Army uniform. His dark and wavy hair tucked under the tiny cap.

My fingers are still against the keys as I come to terms that this can't be in my head. How could I conjure such details, including his birth and death? My body shakes as my brain registers I have been possessed. I have two options, lie down and take it, or fight to free myself. Can I even fight this? What will he do to me if I do? I can't run and hide from him if he's inside me. He's already proved he can make my body do whatever he wants, whenever he wants to do it.

"I'm not some slut you can abuse whenever you want. If you're with me forever, then there are rules, mister. This is my body and you will respect that. No hanky-panky. None. That shit stops as of this moment," I say to my laptop screen.

"When I ask you a question you will tap once for 'no' and twice for 'yes'."

He doesn't respond. I charge on.

"And you will not stop me from finding a way to free you from me. I am not your bride, wife, or lover. You possessed me and I want my life back. Do I make myself clear?"

I yelp when there are two firm taps on my shoulder. My fingers curl and uncurl above the keyboard and every nerve burns like I ran a marathon in five minutes. With my heart racing, and a newfound belief Nathaniel and I are going to get along.

"Good. With that out of the way, time to do some research."

CHAPTER SEVENTEEN

The Diary of Madness

January 7, 2019

Today is the first day of journaling my experiences. I don't know what I expect from this, but I am going to document this journey. Nathaniel kept to his end of the bargain today. Each time I was near Gracey or Richard I was not overcome with fantasies. I spent most of the day buried underneath the estimates for Haven Hill. I did succeed in getting a preliminary budget outline for Richard. He is still cold and distant. Gracey wanted to go out dancing and drinking tonight. I passed, wanting to start my research.

Initial internet browsing is showing nothing of value. How do you Google possession by sex fiend without winding up on Porn Hub? I spent three hours going down the rabbit hole of possessions and how to cure them. Most of it was Hollywood crap, and the little that wasn't was vague or porn and hard to make heads or tails of.

January 19, 2019

Still no leads. Work keeps me busy, ruining all my chances to hit up the library. Gracey was insistent that I needed to relax. I let her drag me to the club last night. I had been trying to avoid the place packed with horny men and women losing all inhibitions. It was amazing. I spent the entire night in the thick of it with Gracey. She always knows how to distract me. That was until it was time to go home.

The two of us shared the backseat of the Uber ride back to my place. We were both riding high on the vibes and a pleasant buzz. I'm not sure what the trigger was. I tried to ignore it. I tried to suppress it. It wasn't until Nathaniel wrapped his arms around me that I could find the center I needed to resist. The fire continued to burn all night. I got no sleep as I kept wanting to fuck Gracey. Especially when she crawled into bed next to me, like she always does after a night of excess.

She acts like nothing's changed between us. I both love and hate it. I want things to be different. Or I think I do. I fear this is a side-effect of Nathaniel, so I don't push to change things between us. Need to experiment further with this whole desire thing to see if Nathaniel is lying to me.

January 20, 2019

I went to church. I was expecting to spontaneously combust the entire time I sat next to my dad. Nothing changed when I took communion. I worked up the courage to take confession after the service and chickened out before I could tell him about Nathaniel. It was awful enough telling the Father about my sexual desires and fantasies. I know the Church's stance on intimacy between women, but I want his blessing to love Gracey. I need it.

Thankfully, the Father is not an old stick in the mud. He didn't condone my feelings for Gracey. He didn't deny them, either. "Love is love." It made me happy to hear. Then he told me to give the standard recitations for the rest of my madness. The prayers did just as much for getting rid of Nathaniel and tamping down my needs as the sermon did.

They're lurking below the surface. If I let my focus slip at all, I start to fantasize. The scenarios my mind conjures are getting wilder and wilder. Thankfully, Nathaniel helps me stave them off. Something about being held by him allows me to center myself and weather the storm.

February 3, 2019

We are getting nowhere. I spent the day in the library flipping through old newspapers on microfilm. I didn't realize that was still a thing. The only common thread that Nathaniel remembers is Haven Hill. The more I dig into that place, the more confused I get. There have always been rumors surrounding it. After the Civil War, it was bought by the Heatherton family. Their daughter, Delores, was Nathaniel's first bride.

Her story isn't well documented. I managed to piece together a few things. Nathaniel helped fill in the holes. The doctors of the time could not help her, and she was forced into an asylum. She committed suicide. Her story makes me doubt the sanity of digging deeper. Nathaniel and I are compiling a list of the other women he remembers, and when I have more free time I will look into them as well.

* * *

February 8, 2019

Gracey wanted to go back out to Onga Bonga tonight. I had to decline. It is impossible to focus. All I want is to feel her, to taste her. Nathaniel suggests that I may need to give in to my wants. He describes it like a dam holding back a river. If you stop the flow, it will back up until it topples the dam and destroys everything. He's suggesting that partaking of the occasional fantasy may help relieve that pent up desire. I'm anxious that if I succumb once, the less likely I am to resist in the future.

He promises me he will help me as best he can. If my alternative is to suffer and be unable to think, then I very well may end up like Delores. I have decided. Tonight, I will let loose and see if it helps. Dear God, please let it help.

February 9, 2019

I feel dirty. It took almost an hour before I was left alone, panting, and exhausted. It took another fifteen minutes before I regained enough composure to bathe myself and change the sheets on the bed. It was as intense as the first night in the mansion. The memory of being used still haunts me. I don't know if I can continue letting the fantasies consume me.

On the other hand, it did allow me to make it up to Gracey. I took her out dancing tonight, and it was amazing. We drank and enjoyed ourselves like before. She is sleeping in the bed while I write this entry. The pull to indulge is minimal. I will have to keep exploring this madness to see if Nathaniel was right. He likened it to a dam blocking a river. This is more like a craving. I need sexual release. I fear if I go too long without it, I will perish. The longer I resist, the dirtier the fantasies become and the more I want them. Could I be in withdrawal?

February 15, 2019

Yesterday was Valentine's Day. I made Gracey take the day off with me and I took her to Hilton Head. She didn't know that was my plan. I had told her I couldn't deal with Richard on the day of love and needed to escape. She agreed without hesitation. We spent exorbitant amounts of money at the shops and danced the night away. Back at the hotel room I decided to make my move.

For weeks I have been watching her, wanting her. I have been indulging in fantasies once every few days to keep my mind from wandering. Every time it involves her and Nathaniel. She has always been there for me, and now I wanted her to know I had seen her. It took a lot more alcohol than I thought it would to build up the courage. I'm not used to being the forward one.

The kiss was amazing. Her reaction was not what I expected. She shied away from me, and asked if we could just snuggle for the night. I tried not to cry in front of her, but the tears came anyway as I faced away from her in the hotel bed. She just held me tighter.

Today was torture. I hate myself for making everything worse. Maybe I do deserve to be all alone, haunted by a sex ghost.

March 1, 2019

I hate everything about Haven Hill. The renovation plans are stuck in a red tape quagmire. Richard is harassing me to finalize the project budget. The more I dig into the history of the house the more bodies I find. I should burn that damn house to the ground and be done with it.

There have been twelve women before me over the last 150 years. Some of them died in tragic accidents. Some committed suicide. Others are missing people, never heard from again, and never will be. As I find information on them, Nathaniel remembers them, and how they died. He refers to every one of them the same way. They were his brides. He only wanted to bring them comfort in their darkest hour. In the end, they always leave him, forcing him back into oblivion while he waits for the next one.

The time he spent with them varies wildly. One woman died the very night he met her. Most lasted weeks to months. Delores lived almost a decade with him. As we delve further into this, we realize he causes their deaths. I am starting to believe him when he says there has to be more to this than just him. If he were malicious, I don't think he would have remorse for their deaths.

It's been two months since I was possessed. I am getting into the top percentile of survivors. I need to figure out how to get rid of him before it's too late.

CHAPTER EIGHTEEN

What a Girl Needs

March 2, 2019

"No. I'm not going to call some huckster TV psychic."

You were the one who said we needed help.

"Yes, help. That doesn't mean some two-bit hack who only wants to scam people out of their money."

How do you know she is a hack? Every time the commercial comes on I can feel you paying attention.

I roll my eyes as I drop the phone onto the couch. "Stop prying. I hate it when you try to guess my feelings."

My hand twitches as he wants to continue the conversation. I don't let him. Nathaniel is quite apt at using a cell phone, and I look less like a crazy person. I chew on my lower lip as I consider his position. He's right, but I'm not telling him that. My research hit a dead end. There is nothing on how he possesses his brides, or how to undo said possessions.

"Fine! You win!" I throw my hands up in mock surrender.

I close the note app I use to chat with him and punch in 1-800-PSY-CHIK. I bet the first thing the automated response will ask for is my credit card number.

"Thank you for calling 1-800-PSY-CHIK." A pleasant voice comes on the line. She doesn't give me time to speak before continuing. "Georgie, she will be there in any moment."

I stare at the screen of my phone after she hangs up on me. My thumb comes to life and pops open the notes again.

What was that? Do you know this woman?

"No," I shake my head, bewildered. "Must be some kind of crazy caller ID nonsense."

She said she was coming here.

"What? No. There's no way she could know I was going to call and leave in time to get he-"

Heavy bangs slam against my front door. The relentless pounding does not stop until I am at the door. I peek through the peephole, hoping that the person on the other side is at the wrong door.

"Are you going to dawdle there all day or open the door?" The woman with the violet eyes from the commercials fisheyes as she leans into the peephole and scolds me.

I gasp as I take a step back. This is freaky, even for a possessed woman.

Nathaniel's hand nudges my elbow.

"Really? You want me to let her in?"

It hardly seems like a coincidence. Maybe she is not a charlatan?

I roll my eyes at the phone and shake my head. I'm going to be the laughingstock of the town when I get rooked by this con artist. I slide the phone into the pocket of my sweatpants and unlock the deadbolt leaving the chain. With my weight against the door, I crack it open. "Can I help you?"

"Yes. Let me in before Mrs. Feinstein calls the cops. We need to talk."

"Really? You expect me to let a complete stranger into my house because you demand it?"

"You're the one who called me, remember? And you also took your sweet damn time doing it, too. I told you to call me back in January, but did you listen? No. You decided to keep playing with that time-bomb in your head. Now, open up!"

I freeze at her claim. I rewound that commercial and confirmed it was Georgia not Georgie.

She raises a brow and cocks her head as if daring me to contradict her.

I ease the door closed and my fingers hesitate over the chain. Nathaniel's hand rests on my shoulder, a sign of comfort. With a dramatic exhale, I slide the chain free and open the door.

"Good." She sweeps past me, hauling a small rolling suitcase behind her. "You consummated yet?"

I blink, my cheeks flaring to life in embarrassment. The door slams as I shut it before my nosy neighbor can butt in. "What?

That's kind of personal. Who are you?"

"Girl, it's a simple question and one with dire consequences. Have you consummated with him?" Her violet eyes dig deep into me, watching, waiting.

My mind whirls. She knows about Nathaniel. Which confirms further he is real and not a figment of my imagination. Or this stranger is stalking me and is here to push me over the edge to steal everything from me.

Nathaniel's hands rest on my shoulders, helping me focus.

"We…have been intimate," I mumble.

She studies me and jumps up from the chair before getting in my face. "That is not what I asked." Her eyes dart side-to-side as she studies me. "Have you consummated? Has he taken your virginity?"

I try to think back to all the encounters with Nathaniel, and struggle. Too many restless nights have gone by for me to remember every intimate moment. A single tap on my shoulder draws the mysterious woman's gaze to it.

"What does that mean? The tap?" She brandishes a finger at my shoulder and hovers close like she's going to devour me for lunch.

"You saw that?" My eyes round like saucers in surprise. No one has even indicated to notice Nathaniel in the past three months.

She glares at me as I fail to answer the question.

"It means 'No.'" I then fish out my phone and ignore her to look at the tiny screen. "What do you mean 'No'?"

All of your fantasies are with me behind you. Gracey is always front and center in your mind.

"Oh." My face burns bright.

The women shifts closer to peer down at my phone, fascinated by our exchange.

"Who the hell are you?" I pull my phone away, not wanting her to invade mine and Nathaniel's private conversation.

"My name is Raven. Everyone calls me Madame, and if the boy is saying you have not consummated, then it is true. Good, then there's a chance."

She turns on heel and tosses her bag onto my island with caring if she damages the finish, unzips it, and flips it open. She fishes through the assorted trinkets in the bag and returns with a compact covered in scratches and holding itself closed with a wish and a prayer.

I shy back from the blue goop on her finger. "What's that for?"

"It is woad. It will help protect. Stop floundering like a fish and let me do my thing."

I hesitate. I don't know this woman from Adam and she wants me to let her put some kind of weird blue stuff on my forehead that she claims will protect me?

Nathaniel taps twice on my shoulder.

I brush my hair out of my face and stand still. If he isn't trying to stop me from interacting with her, he must not sense danger. He explained that there was something evil in that corner and he was trying to protect me at the house where he made me walk backwards.

She dabs the goop on my forehead.

"Yes, she is a handful." Raven cants her head to the side like there is a person standing off to the side she's barking at.

I wonder if that's how I look when talking to Nathaniel.

"Yes, I know I could have come to see her months ago. Until she reached out to me, she wasn't ready." She wheels on her heel and brandishes a woad covered finger at the empty air. "Don't you go getting high and mighty. When they aren't ready it does more harm than good!" She then brandishes the blue-tipped finger at me. "And you, why did it take your sweet time calling?"

"Nuh-uh. You don't get to blame me for not calling a crackpot psychic hotline. Hell, I learned two minutes ago that I'm possessed and not crazy." My back stiffens and I lean in to emphasize my point. My finger juts back at her. "Why didn't you help me?"

She scoffs. "Would you believe me had I come then? You're ready. I'm here. There's much to discuss and too little time." She storms over to the kitchen table and drops into a chair. "Make yourself a cup of tea. I take mine with honey."

"Do I look like a servant? I'm not making you tea." I scoff. The nagging ache between my legs fades and my muscles relax. Breathing becomes easier and the weight on my shoulders lifts. Nathaniel's looming presence remains. What is this woad stuff?

"Georgina Belmont, I am here to help you. When a guest comes you should treat them with kindness."

I huff like a small child at her scolding. I cross my arms to dig in when Nathaniel taps my shoulder once and nudges my elbow. "Fine," I snap at him before I move to my Keurig to make her a cup of tea. "Can-" my question is cut short by her raised hand.

"Tea first."

I serve the tea and sit across from her. "Fine, there's you damn tea. What's going on with me?"

She doesn't answer until after she tastes the tea. The twist of her lips brings a scowl to my face. "You are possessed."

"I've already figured that out. How do I fix it?"

"You don't. The two of you are soul-bonded, meaning you are of one soul. Remove one half and the other will perish." She shrugs.

"I'm stuck with him?"

"Pretty much."

"Then why the fuck did you care if I had consummated with him?" I shout at her and slap the table in frustration.

"Because then you would belong to his Master," she says. She drops the nonchalant attitude. Her gaze darkens as she stares at me over the brim of her teacup, "and that would mean you are a danger to us all. As long as he does not claim your virginity, then there's hope."

"Hope? I thought you said I couldn't get rid of him?" My voice cracks as the frustrated tears well in my eyes. This woman is more maddening than dealing with my desires every ten minutes.

"You are of one soul. That does not mean you cannot prevent this from happening again." She softens as she leans forward. "Georgina, your level of compatibility with him is extraordinary. You must resist the desire, or all is lost." She tilts her head, listening to something I can't see.

"Would you like to meet him?"

I sniffle and rub my eyes with my sleeve. "How is that possible?"

"You still doubt me?" She cracks a grin as she hops up to retrieve a small glass globe from her bag. "This is how."

"A crystal ball?" If I didn't think she was a con-artist before I do now. What is this stuff she put on my forehead? Is it a drug that makes me susceptible to suggestions?

She rolls her eyes at me and sets the small sphere between us. "Give me your hands."

It takes all my willpower to not roll my eyes back at her.

Her hands wait on either side of the ball, palms up.

Nathaniel urges me forward with a gentle tap of my elbow.

An electric tingle passes through me as her hands clamp down like vices onto mine. I wiggle my fingers, trying to regain blood flow.

"Stop fidgeting. This is already hard enough without you breaking my concentration."

All of the discomfort is forgotten when the clear crystal ball fills with cloudy smoke. I yelp and try to pull away.

Madame Raven's grip holds me in place.

A handsome man with wavy brown hair and piercing brown eyes comes into focus. The hazy outline from the mirror is replaced with all the details. His smile is soft and enthusiastic as he gazes back up at me.

"Nathaniel?" My throat constricts and causes me to squeak his name.

Hello, Georgie.

His voice is a rich tenor in my ears.

I stare, transfixed by Nathaniel.

"Is that you?"

Yes, it's me.

"How can I hear you?"

He shrugs and a mischievous grin forms.

My bet is Madame Raven.

"Of course it is me." Raven looks at me like I'm a toddler who said, 'water is wet'. "The two of you were already connecting. It was nothing for me to finish the bridge."

My mind reels under this new circumstance. I never imagined I would be hearing Nathaniel speak. My mind races as I study his small image in the crystal.

He smiles and bows his head.

Georgina, I truly am sorry for what I have done to you. You did not deserve any of this.

My heart is in my throat. The sorrow and regret in his words cause tears to well at the corners of my eyes again. I refused to give him forgiveness when he asked the first day. Nathaniel's calm and steady presence is all that keeps me from losing everything. Any time my body rebelled, he was there to help me resist.

I should forgive him. That's what the Church taught me to do. His words ring in my heart like the bells of Notre Dame, and there's a flutter in my stomach at the emotional need to know I'm not in the wrong. I can't bring myself to say the right words. "I know," I rasp, verklempt.

His sad smile cannot hide the echo of regret and rejection searing through my chest like a hot poker.

"What the...?" I rip my hands from Madame Raven and flinch back.

The image of Nathaniel vanishes from the globe on the table.

"What was that?"

"The bridge between the two of you is strengthening." Raven leans back in her chair, her mocha-colored skin pales, and dark circles form under her eyes. "The more your souls merge, the more powerful it becomes. There is no telling how far your bond will go."

"You mean those were his feelings?" I bring my fist to my chest and hug myself. I hadn't considered he had feelings, or emotions. Until today he was just words in my head with my voice.

"Yes. Georgina, this is dangerous territory you are wandering through. The human body was never meant to carry two souls, even if they are bound and entwined. A time will come where the strain cannot be sustained."

I stare at her, struggling to process her cryptic words. "What does that even mean? Stop with the mumbo-jumbo and just tell me."

She leans forward and jabs a finger at me. "It means you will die, girl." Her tone cuts like a knife and her eyes burn straight into my soul. "Whether it is a traditional death where your father has a body to bury or a spiritual death where your soul is consumed by his is unknown. I have never seen this before. I can feel the dissonance between the two of you."

I fall back into my chair, stunned. My eyes remain fixed on Raven as I try to process her words. "I thought you said there was a chance? That hope remains?"

Hot rage boils deep down in my chest. How dare she string me along. "No. Fuck you. You con artist! I don't know what you did to me. It's bullshit! Get out!"

She draws in a deep breath before launching herself from the chair. She packs the few things she had taken out and zips the suitcase closed. "Girl, your anger at your lot doesn't make me a con artist. The more you fight it, the worse it will be. You don't always get to hear what you want. You have to hear what you need."

I fly out of my chair and storm after her as she heads to the door.

"One last word of warning: Beware the Master." She closes the door behind her.

Warring emotions tie my gut into knots as I try to process everything she said.

Nathaniel wraps his arms around my shoulders and holds me to his chest, trying to comfort me. I lean into it, unsure what to do.

We will continue looking for a way to fight it.

I whirl around as if to look at him. "How can I still hear you? I thought that could only happen while you were in the crystal ball?"

I don't know, but I am glad for it.

Mirth and wonder echo against my disbelief and shock.

"At least you won't have to keep asking to use my hand." I huff, still mad at the strange woman. I stamp my foot in impotent rage. "Whatever. So, what was all that Master nonsense she kept on about?"

I'm not sure. I don't think she is lying. We've both felt it.

"Desire," we both say.

I *thought it was you that drew me to you. I've always believed it was the brides' emotions.*

The ominous sensation of being watched creeps over me. The sudden chill in the room causes me to hug myself and shudder. "There has to be an explanation. Do you remember any other voices with your brides? Or anything that connects everything together? Were they into witchcraft? Did they perform a ritual?"

Sharp pain stabs my temples, like my brain is trying to explode from my skull, and I rub my temples as I stumble to the couch.

Haven Hill…

Nathaniel sounds far away and as if he says more. The words are lost as the pain in my head grows.

"Everything comes back to that damn estate. Oh no!" I have been hyper-focused on my hunt for information into Nathaniel that I neglected my duties at work. The meeting to finalize the plans is on Monday. As my mind shifts to another topic, the pain ebbs in my temples.

You have a whole day to finish your plans. Dick will accept your proposal.

"Richard." I correct him. "His name is Richard."

No, Gracey's correct. He's a dick.

"Nathaniel! I know Richard can be boorish, but he really is a good guy."

Could have fooled me. I've only ever seen him treat you like shit.

Since the start of the new year, I have seen a whole new Richard, and can't argue against Nathanial's point. Not wanting to take relationship advice from the man possessing me, I shift topics, "Do you think Madam Raven wanted to help?"

She's scary, not evil. She was genuinely concerned for you. She is not a charlatan.

"How do you know? All she did was say what we already knew. Well, other than I'm going to die. I wish I never called her."

She also said there was hope. Whatever she did allows us to communicate. I never could talk with my brides before.

"Not your bride." I sigh and curl up on the couch. The anguish of knowing that I am living on borrowed time still gnaws at the back of my mind, but I try to ignore it. Otherwise, I'll end up a blubbering mess and never leave my apartment again.

I promise we will figure this out, Georgina. I won't let you die.

His hand rubs along my back, soothing me. I wish he were real so I could curl into his arms. Once I calm down, I get up and bus the dishes from my impromptu tea party. Under the cup Madame Raven had used is a small business card. I frown at it, expecting it to be the psychic's card, instead it reads, The Bookstore. There's no logo and under the title is an address in Savannah. I flip it over to read, Ask for Khaylia.

How do you even pronounce that name? Why would I take this crazy person's suggestion, even if she knew more of my situation than anyone else in the world. What if this is all part of an elaborate con? Has my father done something terrible to someone and now people like the show Leverage are getting even with me?

We don't have any other avenues to explore. I doubt they are trying to con you. She didn't ask you for anything today. Maybe we should at least investigate this place.

"You want me to go meet up with another wackadoodle?"

Georgie!

His disappointment rails through me worse than one of my father's stony looks.

She came to you when you asked for help.

I huff, wanting to end this conversation. "Fine. I'll think about it."

The card is abandoned on the island as I reclaim my position in front of the TV. I tune out the renovation show in the background as I open the laptop intending to finish my proposal. "What do you remember of the estate?"

Not much. The folks living there were kind enough to offer me a bed and food, and then nothing.

"No, not like that. What do you remember of the house itself? How was it decorated? What colors did they use? Were there specific details that stuck out at you?" I crack open a notepad file to take notes of his details. The thought came to me that if he is from that era, I could at least use his memories to recreate authentic period decorations and give the Historical Society a remarkable place.

Oh. I don't remember much until after the war when I was with Delores. I did get to see most of the main house with her.

My fingers fly over the keyboard as he recounts the details of each room Delores and he ventured into.

CHAPTER NINETEEN

Hope Springs Eternal

March 4, 2019

The sun isn't even up yet by the time I make it into the office. I always do my best work before the bustle of the day pulls me in ten different directions. I hum to myself as I move through the empty office, eager to show Richard my plans for Haven Hill. It has been months of back and forth with both the city and the Historical Society about our plans.

While the architectural aspects are under review, I focus on the interior designs. Nathaniel's insights into how the house used to look were an amazing resource. I should be able to use that as a starting point to bring back the house's former glory.

I pause at the door to my office and frown. Richard was also here early. I glance towards the Gopher pen, glad it is empty. The stares are the worst part. Battle lines were drawn between the women who worked in the cubicles between who supported Richard and who supported me. Every time I have to visit Richard, I can feel their eyes boring into me.

My knock sounds thunderous in the empty office. It's weird how big and lonely an office sounds when no one is around. The tension between my shoulder blades tightens as I hear Richard's muffled shouting. I can't make out what he's saying. I turn to go back to my side of the office when the door is ripped open. "What?" he snarls.

"It's nothing. I'll come back later. You're busy," I rapid-fire apologize and turn to flee back to my office.

His hand is like fire when it catches my wrist. I freeze in place and whip my head around to look at him.

"Let go of me," I say with such authority that I'm not convinced it's me doing the talking.

"Georgie… sorry." His hand drops. "I… are you alright?" His tone shifts to concern and his beautiful green eyes look at me with a softness I haven't seen in a long time.

"I'm fine." I am not in the mood to play twenty questions with Richard. A small part of me wants to tell him everything. The rest of me fears how he will respond.

"Are you sure? You've been acting kind of strange lately. If you want to talk…"

My heart skips a beat. This was the Richard I fell in love with. The kind man with gentle eyes who wanted nothing more than to be with me. I should walk away. This tiny moment of tenderness shouldn't be all it takes for me to forgive him and come crawling back. I truly am pathetic. "Sure. Okay, Richard."

We step into his office.

He closes the door before sitting in one chair on the visitor side of his desk. I fidget with my skirt as I sit across from him. He waits, watching me. This is harder than I thought it would be. My mind wages war on whether to tell him the truth or give him enough to back off. I chew on my lip as I struggle.

"I…" I force myself to take a deep breath. "I'm sorry for claiming you drugged me. The shock of everything that happened over New Year was too much, and I blamed you." I don't look up from my skirt, unable to take his anger.

He shifts in the chair and sits back.

The silence drags on between us for what seems like eternity.

"I'm sorry too, Georgie."

Sadness is etched onto his face when I snap my head up to look at him.

"It was stupid of me to treat you that way." His gaze bounces everywhere in the office except to me. "I could try to make excuses for what I did. I wish you had talked to me about it." His green eyes settle on me. "I've been thinking about this for a while, and I would like us to start over. I miss you. Hell, I even miss Gracey a little too."

My heart is in my throat. This can't be happening. My vision starts to swim with tears threatening to be unleashed. I blink to push them away and draw in a deep breath. He is apologizing. Richard never apologizes.

"I think I would like that."

"Oh? I…" The smile on his face was like the sun coming out from behind the clouds. "I would like that too. Maybe we could start with lunch?"

"Not today. I'm going to be on site with Billy most of this week. I'll text you and we can see where it goes from there, okay?"

"Yeah, that sounds like a plan."

I am on cloud nine as I return to my office. Richard does love me. I want to rip the phone out of my purse and barrage him with messages. We need to take this slow, though, if it is going to work out this time. My thoughts are flooded with the entire checklist of everything I did wrong during our relationship. I sink down into my chair.

Are you sure this is wise?

"What? It's Richard. Of course it is. Like I said, he's a good man. He's sorry for what he did, which means he knows it was wrong. Plus, I'm not an idiot. I will go slow, to make sure."

I still don't like it. That man is a snake oil salesman. You cannot trust him.

"Nathaniel, this is my life. Not yours."

This is our life. This man brings you nothing other than suffering; I don't like how he treats you.

"You don't have to like it, respect that it's my decision."

"Like what?" Gracey's chirp at the door to my office sets my face afire.

"Um…" I flounder for a heartbeat as I try to figure out how long she had been standing there. "Richard."

"You're right, I don't like him." She steps in and sits on the edge of the desk. "What'd he do this time?"

"He apologized."

The shock on her face brings a smile to mine. "He what?"

"He apologized, and asked if we could start over."

"You told him 'No', right?"

"Actually, I told him I was okay with it."

Pain flashes across her face. "Oh… I see."

"We're going to take it slow to start with." My voice is muted. "I still don't trust him, but if there's a chance, I have to take it."

"You need to strike while the iron's hot." She tries to hide the tears by hopping back off the desk and turning her back to me.

I feel like I've been kicked in the gut as she leaves. Am I wrong in trying to patch things up with Richard? I still don't know where I stand with Gracey. Does she want a relationship with me? After Valentine's Day, it's hard to tell what's going on between us. I slip through the hallway and into the women's room to bury myself in a stall and let the tears flow.

Nathaniel holds me as I use toilet paper to dab at my eyes. I don't know what to do now. Gracey's reaction isn't what I expected. She didn't go on a tangent recounting all the reasons to hate Richard and how I could do better. Today she was shattered and retreated like a kicked puppy.

I wait until the bathroom is empty before spending three seconds getting my makeup manageable to hide the tears. I bolt back to my desk, avoiding the inquisitive gazes of the Gophers.

I make sure I am perfect before heading back down to meet up with Billy. His truck is a safe space. I lean against the door and stare out the window.

"Billy? Can I ask you for some advice?"

"Sure, Miss G."

"What do you think of Richard?"

The longer he takes, the more nervous I get that I have overstepped. "Miss G, I think the boy has a good heart, but can be quite the idiot sometimes."

I glance over, surprise bubbling to the surface. That was not the kind of response I was expecting to hear from him. "Really?"

He gives me a small smile. "Really. I've disagreed with some choices he's made, but that doesn't mean he's rotten. Why do you ask?"

"He," I swallow the lump in my throat, "apologized this morning and asked to start over. Should I?"

"Miss G, I think that is between you and your heart. Love is a fickle mistress, and the heart is a mystery at the best of times. If you feel like he is worthy of your forgiveness, then he is worthy. If not, then he ain't. Simple as that."

Nathaniel broods in the back of my mind, unhappy with me even entertaining this thought.

I can picture him sitting there with his arms crossed and his eyes narrowed while his foot taps in agitation.

"Should I forgive him?"

"Up to you, but you shouldn't forget."

I stare at him in confusion as I try to figure out what that means.

"He hurt you and betrayed your trust, Miss G. Forgiveness does not mean a blank check back to the way things were before."

I nod. Nathaniel's smug agreement sparks anger. Why does everyone except me hate Richard so much?

"Thanks, Billy. I'll keep that in mind."

CHAPTER TWENTY

A Monster in Man's Skin

March 8, 2019

I haven't been this nervous since Richard first asked me out in high school. The pristine racks of blouses and pencil skirts taunt me as I stare at them. Gracey wanted to donate them all to Goodwill, but I couldn't bring myself to part with them. The memories of Richard lighting up every time he sees me in one of them is enough to keep them. Today, I am happy I made that decision.

While I wear them for him, they are uncomfortable. I hate how they restrict my movement. I would much rather wear a nice flowing dress with pockets. My hands flex open and closed as I deliberate.

You should wear the blue dress you got. It makes you happy.

I sigh. "It's not that... Richard prefers clothing that shows off my figure. I want to look my best tonight."

My fingers trail along the shimmery fabric of a cocktail dress hanging next to skirts. This is dinner. That level of dress is overkill, but I'm positive he would love it. I chew on my lip.

Then I still stand with my suggestion.

I roll my eyes as he bumps me with his shoulder in jest. His amusement is tinged with worry and something darker I can't quite put my finger on. He has a point. If Richard has changed, I should be able to wear what I want him to see me in.

I turn to look at the dresses hanging behind me. These are the dresses that Gracey and I picked during our retail therapy sessions. An ache forms in my chest as Gracey's smoldering gaze in the dressing room flashes before me.

Georgie?

"It's nothing."

I shake my head to dismiss the memories, but the ache lingers. It's not like Gracey and I are a couple. She said she was okay with me going on this date. Well, almost okay. She's still upset with Richard.

I settle on the dress that Nathaniel suggests. I spend the rest of the time primping in the mirror to make sure my makeup is perfect.

Richard leans against a sleek black muscle car, the top button of his dress shirt undone and his dark suit jacket open to show off his physique. My heart jumps into my throat as I see him. His dark hair is unruly in the breeze. His gaze wanders from head to toe as I approach.

He pulls me into a tight hug. My arms slip around him, as I drink in his warmth. His cologne soothes my nerves.

"You're stunning. When did you get that?" He steps back to arm's length, his hands comforting on my shoulders. A smile flits across his lips as his eyes scan my outfit. "Shaking things up, I see. You always dress to impress."

"Thank you." My heart flutters at the wash of compliments. He has changed and everyone else is incorrect.

The car rumbles and purrs as he speeds along. It brings back memories of us racing through the night, escaping to a secluded spot for hours.

You can still cancel. I'm sure Gracey would be more than happy to meet you at the restaurant.

I squash my annoyance at Nathaniel and smile at Richard. "I like the new car."

"Yeah?" Richard glances over towards me. "Me too. The insurance payout helped cover the down payment on this guy."

I enjoy the patter of his voice. I don't care about the car or the specifics, but the way his face lights up as he talks is worth everything. His entire demeanor is different. He looks relaxed and open as he uses his hands to articulate what he's saying.

We pull up to his favorite Italian restaurant and he tosses the valet the key before coming around to open the car door for me. This is what it is supposed to be like. I hated all the yelling and screaming and nasty remarks.

We're seated in a back corner booth after a brief wait, and the maître d' even welcomes us by name.

I browse the menu as we wait.

The server is at our table within minutes and fills our glasses with water. "Welcome. My name is Raquel and I will be your server tonight. Would you like to hear our recommended vintages?"

A spark of jealousy flashes to life as Richard smiles in a far-too-familiar fashion at the server. I shove it back down into the dark hole it came from. He isn't flirting. This is the way Richard has always behaved.

"Thank you, Raquel. We will start with antipasto misto, then move to minestrone. For the salad, let's do Ceasar. Then we'll have the piccata de pollo with fettuccine alfredo and finish the night with tiramisu. We would also like a bottle of Merlot."

The server collects the menus and bustles off to fulfill his request. I deflate a little but force a smile. I was eyeing the ravioli and tortellini dishes, but he ordered before I could decide.

Rude.

I try to shush Nathaniel as I turn my attention back to Richard. It doesn't matter. All of the food in the place is delectable.

"Richard-"

"I-"

We try to talk simultaneously and share a small laugh. "You go." I wave for him to speak.

"Georgina, I have been a real idiot." He reaches across the table and takes my hands. "I don't deserve your forgiveness. I've hurt you. I'm sorry." He pauses as he struggles to go on. "You know how I get when I get stressed. I was trying to work through some shit and took it out on you."

I am still trying to process my emotions and the server returns with the wine. I cover my lack of response with pleasantries and examining the wine. The red smells sharp and pungent to me. I prefer Moscato.

He waits for the area around us to be clear again before continuing. "I've realized how much I love you Georgie, and I hate that I drove you such extremes."

My fork hovers mid-bite, an olive threatening to roll off the prongs as my hand trembles. I shove it in my mouth to cover my shock by chewing. He said he still loves me. I finish the salty bite of meat and olives before looking up into his hopeful eyes.

He also said you were the extreme one. Was he not the one who cheated and drugged you?

"I love you too, Richard. I wanted none of this either," I reply as tears cling to my lashes.

"I know, Georgie, I know." He takes my free hand in his. "Can you find it to forgive me? Put all your anger behind you and move forward with me?"

You should be angry, Georgina. He should respect your wishes and never put you in that situation to begin with.

Nathaniel doesn't understand. I fly off the handle and am emotional. Richard's the level-headed one and that he understands me and still wants me is all I ever wanted. "Oh, Richard. Of course I forgive you."

Mistrust and suspicion float through the back of my mind, which I attribute to Nathaniel being jealous. I focus on Richard and the joy I am experiencing. A small niggle of guilt bubbles to the surface as I realize I am going to have to tell Gracey.

"Good. I was worried you had worked yourself into such a state you could never come back to me." His smile softens, and he releases my hand to dig into his own appetizer.

He should be worried. He doesn't deserve you, Georgie.

I close my eyes, trying to tune out Nathaniel before I eat. Frantic to make this date perfect, my stomach was too twisted to allow me to eat prior.

The drive home is pleasant, and Richard holds my hand the entire time. The smile on his face is carefree and draws out his sweet dimples. He pulls into the parking lot of my building and puts the car in park.

"I had a lovely time tonight," he says as he faces me.

"Me too."

He leans in, his hand coming up to cup my neck and draw me closer to meet him.

The sweet scent of his cologne surrounds me and his fingers are warm against my skin. My eyes flutter closed and our lips meet. The kiss is sweet and tender at first, two new lovers testing the waters.

Encouraged by my sigh, Richard deepens the kiss.

We part and both bite against our lower lip, smiling like fools. This is just like the first night in that closet.

"You want to come up?"

I don't think that's a good idea, Georgina. You wanted to take this slow. If he comes up, he's going to think you're wanting more.

"Really? I would love that," Richard's beaming smile as he kills the engine makes my heart sing.

I ignore Nathaniel's anger and worry, not wanting to lose this warm and fuzzy feeling of Richard being happy with me. I ease out of the car and we walk hand in hand to the door of my building.

Richard turns me and kisses me again, pressing me against the door. His hands roaming over my sleek dress until he cups my ass and squeezes. His lips trail away from mine and along my jaw until he nibbles on my ear. "I want you," he whispers.

The light teasing is enough to send sinful jolts of desire along my skin, causing me to grind against him in needy lust.

"That's my girl," he murmurs as his kisses continue and he guides a leg up along his hip.

My chest rises and falls with my heavy breathing, and I lace my fingers into his hair, encouraging his sweet kisses. I want more. I need more. I ache for his touch and my clothes are burning against my skin with the flames of my wanton desire.

Nathaniel's one hand cups my breasts and squeezes as he

presses from behind. His manhood is hard against my ass. His lips brush along my neck opposite of Richard. His other hand slides down to rub me through my dress. The timid warning of his affection gone, and he's rough in reminding me he wants me as much as Richard does.

For a few blissful seconds I'm held between the man I've always wanted and the man I'm bound to and everything is right in the world. They're all I need.

Desire. The saccharine female voice is alien and dreadful as it echoes through my mind.

My eyes fly open and fear floods ice into my veins. I tense in Richard's arms, squirming to escape his and Nathaniel's touch. "No," I whimper.

"No?" Richard pulls back and furrows his brow down at me. "What do you mean, no?" His tone shifts from lustful and tender to edging on anger.

Nathaniel's touches cease. His presence is heavy and wanton. The mix of jealousy and desire slams against my lust and panic.

"Richard, I..." My throat constricts as I struggle to wrestle with my emotional nightmare. I shake my head, failing to communicate to him how afraid I am.

He pushes from me and runs his fingers through his hair. "Are you fucking kidding me, Georgina? I do everything for you and you're going to fucking tease me again? Was this your plan all along? Lure me back in and string me along? For what? You're sick, you know that."

"No, Richard, please. No. It's not that, I swear. I want to. I do. I just…" I cling to him in desperation. "Something's happening to me." The waterworks flow and the dam of keeping Nathaniel to myself cracks. "I'm having all these feelings and sensations, and then this thing with Gracey, it's-."

"I fucking knew it! You've been her little slut all this time and when she threw you away you decided to come crawling back to me. Is that it?" He pries my hands from him and steps out of reach.

Rage wells like a bull ready to charge the matador as Nathaniel's presence overwhelms me.

I shake, unable to contain the whammy of emotions between Nathaniel and myself.

"Richard, please," I beg.

His jaw clenches and he stares at me long and hard. The cold and unloving gaze replaced the sweet man I fell in love with again. "I'm going to go before you make me regret this. You need to think long and hard, Georgie. If you want me in your life, you need to make the right choices of who else you keep in your life. I love you. But I won't tolerate being so ill-treated."

He walks away, not waiting for my response.

He won't tolerate this?! How dare he. Oh, that I had my body! I would show him how a man acts. You are the light of the sun, Georgina. He should be worshiping the ground you walk on and be grateful you even give him a passing glance. Your heart is full of love. You are the kindest soul I have ever met. He is a monster for treating you like this! Let me, Georgina. Let me at him. I will make him rue the day he ever hurt you.

Richard's car peels out of the parking and I hug myself, rooted to the spot where he left me. Nathaniel's rant rings in my ears and I'm more confused. His emotions batter against me like a hurricane. Anger, frustration, sadness, and love. How could Nathaniel love me? He's a ghost.

I'm not a ghost.

"You're dead. You said so yourself. There is a death certificate for you."

It does not change my emotions. Georgina, I have never connected with any of my brides as I do with you. Not even Delores. You're special. With them, I existed and fulfilled their desires. With you, I… I want to hold you and kiss you. I want to sit with you on the couch and eat ice cream. I want to help you rebuild houses. This torture pains me. Only being allowed to make you feel what I can give you. I want more. I want to live. I love you, Georgina.

I look at my hands, my chest rising and falling with the labor of breathing. This is too much to handle all at once. Richard has me all in knots and worried I have ruined everything again. Gracey's still being weird, and now Nathaniel's professing his love for me.

"I…I need to be alone."

Pain clutches my chest when Nathaniel's presence disappears. Hollowness replaces the warmth of his emotions. I know as soon as he's gone it was the wrong choice, again. I drive everyone away. There is something wrong with me. How could Nathaniel love me?

CHAPTER TWENTY-ONE

Dreams Are a Nightmare Your Heart Makes

The club hums with the throngs of people bumping and grinding to the loud German music I can't understand. Gracey's smile is infectious as she throws her hands in the air to groove. I mimic her and our wild dancing draws us closer.

Sweat soaked and panting, the strobing lights bounce off our sparkling dresses, creating a technicolor rainbow of lights around us. The crowd fades, and music dulls until all that remains are the two of us.

Her soft lips brush mine and taste like cherries.

In the blink of an eye our clothes are gone and we're on a bed covered in satin sheets. Gracey hovering over me like a blue-haired goddess before she dips her head to draw one of my nipples between her teeth.

I arch and cradle her head, encouraging her to continue. The biting sting of her attention causes me to breathe harder and grow *wetter. I lift my head to watch her crawl backwards over me.*

She smirks as her lips leave butterfly kisses along my stomach until she noses my thighs further apart. Her tongue flicks along my tender flesh and I shudder.

When she hesitates, I mewl, begging for more.

"So needy," she purrs, her hot breath washing over me. Her tongue delves between the folds as her finger presses into me, leaving me no time to respond,.

I grip the sheets and rock up to meet her.

Her chuckle tickles me and she devours me like she's starving.

My body shudders with my orgasm. Every nerve afire with sensation.

Gracey doesn't stop there, trailing soft kisses up my stomach until she draws me into a fiery kiss. Her tongue pressing my mouth open and forcing me to taste myself on her.

I moan and cling to her. Her affection is divine and what love should be. I never want this to end.

"It doesn't have to," she murmurs against my lips as she leans up. The tattoos that vine her body spring to life, rising out of her skin to surround us.

"Gracey?" I whimper.

"I need you, Georgie. All of you," her husky voice is graveled and foreign, not like the sweet melodious tones I'm used to. "He needs you." She turns me, the vines twisting around us until I'm facing Nathaniel.

His intense brown eyes gaze at me. His lips are parted and his toned chest rises and falls. "I love you, Georgina," he murmurs as he leans in and draws me into a tender kiss, nothing like the sinful kisses Gracey plants me with.

Gracey shifts behind me, pressing me to Nathaniel's naked body, her vines curling along my sides and over his hips to engulf us both. "We need you, Georgie," her voice coos in my ear.

"Yes," I whine against Nathaniel's lips.

His smile is like the sun chasing away the clouds as his rough hands grope my breasts.

The vines wrap around my legs, pulling them apart as the bed disappears and we float in an ethereal plane of stars. Gracey's hands slide along my arms, raising them above my head until vines bind my wrists together, holding me open to the two of them.

Nathaniel shifts and the thick smooth head of his cock brushes along me, sending shivers up my spine.

My clit throbs faster than a rave beat, and I squirm in futile efforts to draw him in.

He takes hold of my hips in one hand and guides his cock in with the other, the slow pressure drawing an illicit moan from me. This isn't like before, and hurts, his cock is too large, pressing deeper and deeper until he gives a quick thrust, burying himself deep.

From behind, Gracey nibbles on my ear, her breasts pressing into my back, only one of her vines presses against my ass, and forces itself in to match Nathaniel.

My strangled yelp is muffled by the consuming kiss Nathaniel draws me into. He cups my ass as he pumps hard and steady into me.

Gracey cups my breasts and tweaks my nipples while she pumps from behind me, her vine swelling and filling me until I believe I'll be split in two.

The coppery scent of blood fills my nostrils and fear overtakes enjoyment as I struggle to free myself. Their lovemaking turns to fucking as Nathaniel's eyes blaze with lust.

His cock swells and then erupts like a volcano inside of me.

I gasp awake, sitting up to find myself in my bed, alone. My clit throbs and my heart pounds in my chest. Sweat covers my skin. With trembling fingers I reach between my legs and yelp. Everything is swollen and sensitive and when I bring my fingers up to inspect them, the hint of blood mixes with my cum.

"What the fuck," I whisper. What have I done? How is this possible? Raven warned me not to consummate my relationship with Nathaniel. She said to be wary of the Master, but never explained and I haven't spoken to her since. I stare at my fingers covered in blood and cum, unable to comprehend what happened.

Nathaniel's arms wrap around me and he nuzzles me.

We are husband and wife.

"What?" I shriek and try to escape the bed, only to be held in place by him.

Georgina, you gave yourself to me. We completed the bond. I am yours and you're mine. As you desired.

His voice changes and hisses with the tinges of the feminine voice.

The spot on my forehead where Raven dabbed that goo burns.

"Oh God," I wail. "No. No, no no. This isn't happening. No."

I'm sorry, Georgina. I could not stop myself. I only want to make you happy.

Nathaniel's voice is back to normal. It doesn't matter. I'm in over my head. I need help. There's only one person I can trust and she'll know what to do. I should have told her sooner. Panicked it's too late, I reach for my phone to call Gracey.

Six unread messages from Richard await me.

As is an entire conversation I don't remember having with him.

You up?
No.

Funny. Can we talk?

No.

Don't be like this Georgie. I just want to talk.

To berate me and treat me like the philanderer you are. No, sir.

C'mon, G. I need you.

What you need is a swift kick in the ball sack and for someone like Mr. Coeh to put you through a wall.

Why are you being weird? What the fuck? Jesus, I was trying to say I wanted you to come over and work things out.

By working them out, you mean abuse me further and take advantage of my fragile state so you can remain in good graces with my father?

You don't have to be a cunt. You're the one who was in my office begging me to fuck you earlier. And no. I need someone to talk to about important shit.

Then find yourself a doctor, you jackass. You had the perfect gift in this divine creature and blew it by not being patient. She moved on and found a loyal man.

Gracey, quit being a bitch and give the phone to Georgie.

No. This is not Gracey.

I know you're not fucking, Georgie. Who are you?

Nate

WTF?!?! Georgie, who the fuck is Nate? Are you seriously already fucking someone else? I thought you loved me? Answer me! Quit fucking around!

My chest tightens like a corset was laced too tight. I can't breathe as all my emotional markers fly out the window. Why is this happening to me? My entire world is crashing down around me. Nathaniel told Richard about him while I was sleeping. How is that possible when he was raping, no not rape. I said yes. Oh

God, I said yes. My heart thunders like war drums in my ears. What am I going to do?

"No, no, no," I say, hysteria sending my voice higher in pitch with each denial.

I'm sorry, Richard. I was drunk. Please don't hate me. I don't know what got into me.

As my thumb hovers over the send button, my entire arm trembles like I'm holding a thousand pound weight in it.

"Are you fucking kidding me?" I shriek at my phone.

My fingers move, only they don't hit send. A thundering in my ears builds as I realize Nathaniel's stopping me from sending my plea.

I told him the truth. He doesn't deserve you! You are too special to keep being abused by that louse.

Flames of rage burning in my chest make focusing more difficult.

"YOU DON'T MAKE THAT DECISION FOR ME!"

You are mine. I will not idly stand by and let another man besmirch your honor. He is lucky I do not beat him to within an inch of his life for how he treated you.

Richard, for all his terrible words, is the only person I thought loved me. My father doesn't love me. Gracey will never love me after this.

The thought of her and I being together flushes my cheeks. Loving another woman is a sin by the laws of the church. I'm a walking pile of shame and deserve Richard and all his hate.

NO! Georgina, you deserve love and adoration. You are kind and caring. You try to please everyone around you, even at your own expense. I am sorry this happened to you. I will no longer allow you to suffer that monster. I will always defend and protect you. Now that we have consummate our union, there is nothing I won't do to honor and cherish you, even if that means protecting you from yourself.

"Get the fuck out of my head!"

I rear back to throw my phone at the wall, only my hand won't release it. I scream in frustration. "You don't own me! This is my body! My life! You are a fucking demon-ghost-whatever and can't to do this to me!"

Electricity hums through the room like a gospel chorus singing backup in this melodrama. The lightbulb in the lamp on my nightstand shatters. A giant spark rips through me, every nerve alive with pain.

I am not a demon! Like it or not, we are bound until you die. I don't understand why, or how it happens. Raven told you fighting will only make it worse. You need to calm down.

"Calm down?! Did you just fucking telling me to calm down? I'm fucking possessed! I didn't ask for you to bind your soul to mine. Get the fuck out, or so help me, I-."

The pain increases beyond any I've experienced before. Like a hot knife flays the skin from my body, and a giant, wicked cheese grater shreds my soul to pieces.

A strangled cry rips from my throat. I crumple to the floor, gritting my teeth and curling into a ball. Black spots blur my vision. A jet engine level of ringing drowns out any other noises.

"Please… Stop. Don't murder me." I whimper before succumbing to unconsciousness.

******

I admit I crossed a line in responding to Dick. I never thought she would unleash her wrath on me for defending her. Thankfully, she cannot hurt me.

As she roars at me, her heart beats harder and faster. The strange sensation of being pushed frightens me. My brides have never been capable of connecting with me in such a fashion.

Raven's warnings ring in my head.

I am not a demon! Like it or not, we are bound until you die. I don't understand why, or how it happens. Raven told you fighting will only make it worse. You need to calm down.

Telling her to calm down has the opposite effect of what I desired. The light explodes and pain tears through my chest as if my heart is being ripped from its cradle.

This beautiful girl has done something to me. This time is different. There's a connection between us I can't explain. In the few short months of being bound to her, I want nothing more than to be corporeal and to hold her to me. The hours I have spent scouring the internet while she sleeps for an answer have proved in vain. Before tonight I wanted to cross the line and reach out to Raven again. Or to contact The Bookstore. Anything to make Georgina's suffering come to an end and the two of us to have a happily ever after.

She hits the floor. Her heart jackhammers too hard for her body.

As the seconds tick by a numbness creeps up my ankles, giving me the wrong impression that I'm floating. This always happens before I'm forced to return to the mansion. "No!"

I force her lungs to draw air and her muscles to relax, again violating the agreement to not overtake her. She will forgive me, provided she survives. The fog grows thicker around me, threatening to sever our bond.

Georgina's accusations ring in my ears. I am murdering this

wonderful woman. Am I no better than the demon she claims to me to be?

What is it your desire?

The feminine voice whispers through the cloud.

"No! You go away. I will not let you take her!" I wave my arm like I could chase away the approaching thief.

Georgina is my body and soul. She must live.

My entire world crashes to a halt as the thundering of her blood flowing through her veins stops. No steady thump, no whisper of air drawn. Nothing. Georgina lies limp on the floor. A tsunami of panic drowns me for a fleeting heartbeat.

"Oh God!"

I rest my hand on her chest. I curl my fingers around her heart and delicately squeeze. The muscles react to my pressure.

I cannot save her on my own, forcing me to split my focus to text for help.

"Come on, Georgie, breathe. Help is on the way, I promise."

With the message sent, I continue massaging.

"Okay. She is not breathing on her own. Lungs. Need to make the lungs expand."

I inhale, and her chest rises as air fills her lungs, neglecting the other vital action.

"Shit. Heart too. Breathe and heart. Breathe and heart."

As I chant the mantra, her body pantomimes life. Her heart weighs heavy in my hands as the blood begins to flow in time to my actions.

Minutes tick by like hours.

The fog recedes, allowing me to channel all my energy on keeping my girl alive.

"Please, God. I'll do anything if you save her."

Is this what you desire?

"Fuck you. Go the fuck away. This is all your fault." I yell into the void, my eyes never leaving Georgie.

As you wish, Nathaniel.

I ignore the taunting voice and find the rhythm to keep her from perishing. Her body is not acting of her own volition. Soon, I'll be forced to face the truth. I murdered another innocent girl. I am a monster. How could I do this to these women?

My pace creeps with the crushing doubt of not being able to save my Georgina.

"No! I will not lose this one too!"

I wrap my arms around her and continue to make her body respond. I press to her, and my heart slows. My chest rises and falls with hers. Where she begins and I end melds. I refuse to accept her death and keep her with me.

"Please don't leave me. I need you. We belong together. If you come back, I promise, I will only ever act by your command."

CHAPTER TWENTY-TWO

Do You Feel Safe at Home?

Five Days Later

The cold air amplifies the stench of rubbing alcohol. The last thing I remember was screaming at Nathaniel for taking control without my consent. My arms and legs are like lead pipes attached to me, and my lower back hurts.

What is that ticking? It's not a clock, and it doesn't match the beeping sound. Wait, is that a heart monitor? Where am I?

I begin to register I'm in a medical room of some sort. The ticking is out of place.

Is that a rosary? Is this what the pearly gates are like? Did that bastard kill me?

No.

Nathaniel's no is faint, like he's far away. As angry as I am with him, I find comfort in knowing he wasn't trying to kill me.

Am I crazy that I wanted you to answer?

No.

A phantom hug engulfs me, though it's muted compared to before.

"Hail Mary, full of grace." My father's voice murmurs somewhere near the edge of my bed. The tick follows his "Amen."

Why is he saying Hail Mary? Am I dying?

No.

Are you lying?

No.

What's with the one-word answers? What's wrong with you?

Pain.

You feel pain? Where am I? What did you do to me?

I grunt my displeasure when he doesn't respond to me. His presence is weak. Which brings a whole new level of anxiety to me. The memories of our last fight filter through my confusion. I have no time to dwell on the tangled ball of emotional trauma between us when my name's called.

"Georgina?" The gritty, hoarse voice sounds more like a panhandler than my ever-perfect father.

I force a thousand pound eyelid to crack open.

"Georgina!" My father takes my hand and squeezes.

The searing pain of his gesture causes me to groan. Other than soreness, I feel like Billy hit me with his pickup, then backed over me to hit me again.

"Hang on, baby, I got you."

The room morphs from serene to chaos in mere moments.

My father's hand slips from mine as an entourage of nurses and doctors surround me like an inquisition.

"Can you open your eyes?"

"What is your name?"

"What's the date?"

"Can you squeeze my fingers?"

"You know," I rasp. "Rapid-fire questions are hard to answer. Daddy?"

"I'm here, baby. You're going to be okay."

"Miss Belmont, I need you to answer my questions."

"Maybe you should ask them one at a time," I mutter as I open my eyes to look at the man bothering me.

A man in a crumpled shirt with scruffy stubble, disheveled hair, and dark circles around his eyes hovers in the background. I try to talk to the ghost of a man that is my father when the rude doctor blocks my line of sight.

"What is your name?" He asks his question as a demand.

"Georgina."

"Good. What's the date?" He scribbles on his clipboard and it sounds like nails on a chalkboard.

"How the fuck would I know, I was asleep."

Laughter from the peanut gallery causes me to smile up to Dr. Asshole.

"Charming," he says with a deadpan glare. He holds out his fingers. "Squeeze, please."

"Most guys at least offer me dinner before they ask me to tug on them."

The Herculean effort to lift my arms and grip his fingers is answered with a grunt. As a reward for my compliance, he blinds me with a pen light.

"Hmm." He scribbles something else on his paper.

"Hmm," I mimic.

"Well, it appears you are going to recover."

"Recover from what?"

"You had a myocardial infarction."

I stare at him, unable to process the medical gibberish.

"A heart attack. Thankfully, the damage is minimal, and it looks like you will fully recover. We're going to run some tests to confirm before releasing you to your father's care."

"I'm fine." I try to lift my hand to wave them off. "I don't need to go with him."

"Georgina," my father chastises. "This is not the time."

"Miss Belmont, You have been unconscious for five days after suffering a heart attack. It would be better if you had someone to help you rest and recuperate."

"You said I was fine," I whine.

"It isn't normal for a woman your age to have this kind of episode." He pauses and looks over his shoulder. "Please show Mr. Belmont out."

The room falls silent as the nurses usher my father out, leaving me with Dr. Asshole and one nurse.

"This is a safe place, Miss Belmont. Anything you say will be kept confidential. Did you ingest anything before you passed out?"

"No. I was shouting at my boyfriend."

"Do you feel safe enough to go home?"

He thinks something nefarious happened to me. I have half a mind to tell him what Nathaniel did. Images of Sucker Punch dance through my head, and not the fun parts where they're dancing to music.

"I'm fine at home."

"I see." His brows scrunches, making him look like a bulldog turned human. "Have you been under a lot of stress?"

I snort. *Stress? Yes, doc. I smashed my fiancé's car because he was fucking his assistant. And now I'm possessed by a hot Civil War guy who turned me into his own personal sex toy. Oh, and I found out I'm in love with a chick.* "Just work stuff."

"Have you been experiencing episodes of overwhelming sadness?"

It's my turn to make the bulldog expression as all the pieces of what he's asking me fall into place.

"No. I didn't try to kill myself. Like I said, I was screaming at my boyfriend and then everything went black until I woke up here to the Spanish Inquisition."

The nurse chuckles. "Well, it's never expected, honey."

Dr. Asshole's eyes narrow as he cuts the nurse a scowl.

"We're going to keep you for one more night for observation. It's your decision. I strongly recommend you have someone stay with you for a few days."

Sure, pal. I told you I had a boyfriend. He's with me twenty-four-seven and totally isn't the reason I'm here. He only tried to ruin my life and make me text horrible things to my ex who he thinks is a louse.

Husband. Funny.

The clear sarcasm from Nathaniel makes me giggle. I don't miss his husband comment. I can't unpack that bag of crazy with Dr. Asshole hovering over me. I cough to recover my serious face. "Fine. I'll go with my father."

"Good," he forms the hint of a smile as his tone turns less drill sergeant and more arrogant jerk, "I'll get the tests started."

He leaves the room, his nurse in tow. The homeless man playing the role of my father enters.

"How you feelin', sweetheart?"

Who is this guy? Now he cares? "Fine."

"Fine is a four-letter word."

Yep. There's my father.

We stare at each other. The high noon whistle blows through my mind, and I half expect a tumbleweed to roll between us.

"I don't want to be a burden."

"Burden? You're my daughter. You've never once been, nor will you ever be a burden." He stuffs his rosary beads in his pocket as he comes closer.

"Is that why you sent me to boarding school faster than a speeding bullet?"

My father winces, as if I slapped him. "It was the best opportunity for you."

"Right. Then why didn't you leave me there?"

"Circumstances changed, and you were needed here."

"Needed here? You needed your teenage daughter you hadn't seen in years to the point you ripped her from everything she had?"

"Yes. This is your home and where you belong."

"No. This is your home. Mine was an over-priced all-girls boarding school. What did I do that made you hate me this much?"

This is the same argument we have had since he brought me home. He'll tell me I'm dramatic and he doesn't hate me. I will say, you must because you always screw up my life as you see fit. Then he's going to roll his eyes. I'll start to cry. He'll hug me and try to placate me.

I lie there, waiting for his same old response, wishing my arms were not made of lead so I could cross them in a sulking fit.

His clenched jaw twitches, and his skin reddens, adding to his mad-man appearance. Deep breaths make his nostrils flare like a bull staring down a red cloak.

Yup, he hates me.

He does not.

You stay the fuck out of this.

I will not.

I open my mouth to save us the song and dance when the dance changes. My father deflates like a bouncy castle that popped a hole. His jaw unclenches, his shoulders droop. He sighs and slumps into the chair behind him.

"Georgina, I'm sorry. I've always loved you and will always love you. I sent you to that boarding school to protect you." He pauses.

For the first time in my life, my father has no comeback. The hesitation in his voice sets off warning bells louder than the Cathedral of Notre Dame. I swallow hard, and guilt makes my body tense, reminding me of how much pain I'm in.

"Our home was no longer safe. I sent you there because it took you out of danger. When it was safe, I brought you home. Because I need you here."

"In danger, how?" I'm reluctant to let all these years of angst go with one apology.

"Nothing for you to worry about. The threat is long gone."

His stoic, noncommittal face returns, making me want to scream.

Don't do it.

I'm getting really sick of you men telling me what I need and don't. He fucking lied to me for years.

"Why didn't you tell me the truth?"

"I wanted you to live your life without that cloud of fear. I want you to have the best life. If giving you that means you hate me, I'm willing to pay that price." Tears well in his eyes. "With the thought of losing you, lying to you is no longer an option."

My heart monitor beeps increase in speed, giving away my true feelings. I wrack my brain, trying to remember what happened before he sent me away. All I can remember is the funeral, then being put on a plane. "Then quit avoiding and tell me what the extreme danger was?"

His eyes lock on mine.

The longer he delays, the heavier the blanket of dread becomes, whispering that he's going to tell me I have always been possessed by Nathaniel.

He puffs air out like a steam engine and says one word.

"Vampires."

CHAPTER TWENTY-THREE

I Will Remember You

My fingers curl into the sheets. Pain radiates along my jaw and down my neck from grinding my teeth. Of all the lies my father could tell, he chooses to mock me with something beyond fantastic.

"Sure. Vampires, whatever you have to tell yourself to sleep at night. Get out." I grip the sheets tighter and nod towards the door.

My father has the gall to frown and stare at the floor like he's the victim here. Like he didn't take my raw and honest plea to understand why he hates me this much and stomp all over it like he's squishing a cockroach.

Tears blur my vision and I look away from him. The heart monitor I'm chained to gives away my distress.

"Georgina." His voice cracks. "Look at me."

As much as I don't want to give him anything, I glare at him, refusing to back down.

"The summer before I sent you to London, you were out chasing fireflies with your mother. I…was not there. Off doing something stupid." His Adam's apple bobs as he swallows hard and looks down at his hands. "By the time I found you, your brother was already turned, and your mother was dead. I did… what I was trained to do." He rubs his hand as if it is cramped. "Your mother died saving you."

"Stop it!" I scream. "Vampires aren't real! If that's what happened, why don't I remember any of it?" Rage blinds me from seeing any truth in his words. White hot pain courses through my veins. How could my father be like this to me? Why can't he tell me the truth? What happened to my mother and brother that would make him hate me this much?

My father keeps staring at his hands, his voice eerie in its calmness. "You were having nightmares and not sleeping." He rubs his hand harder, fidgeting with his wedding ring. "Your screams echoed throughout the house." He swallows hard and meets my gaze. "I turned to The Collector, a powerful fae. I had him fix you."

"Fixed? Like gluing a fucking porcelain-."

The room tilts. Piercing pain stabs between my eyes; the agony travels up over my skull.

Too many inputs overlap at once.

The panic beeping of my heart monitor.

Nathaniel calls my name.

My father parrots him from a different plane.

Until they all fade away.

Relaxing silence envelopes me. The fresh scent of fresh cut grass. Steamy Savannah summer heat washes over me.

* * *

******

"Momma! See! They light up!"

"They sure do!"

"Can we keep them?"

"Would you like to live in a jar the rest of your life?" She squats down, holding her hand out. The little bug crawls across her finger, his light shining bright.

"No!" I giggle.

Momma's head swivels toward the wall.

"Tyler! Run!" She snatches my hand and drags me toward the house.

"Ow! You're hurting me! Momma! Stop!" My weak resistance is futile in the fury of her pace.

Momma freezes and shoves me behind her.

I peek out from around her skirt to see a strange man blocking our way. Everything about him, his square jaw, his cruel grin, his hollow eyes, send shivers through me despite the heat.

"Awe, sugar. Ain't no reason ta be rude," the man growls. "Dis ain't no way to treat yer guests."

"Mom! Help!" Tyler shrieks. He's flailing and kicking in the arms of another scary looking man.

Not wanting to see, I bury my face against Momma's leg.

"No! Please! He's only a child!"

"Maybe dat hunter prick shoulda thought o' dat 'fore he done murdered my cousin. Tell me 'bout this pretty little thing. Bet she tastes mighty sweet."

I peek up from her skirt to see the scary man moves around us.

"Go fuck yourself." Momma puts her hand on me and turns in a circle while keeping me against her.

"Oh, darlin'! I plan on fuckin' much more dan dat."

In a quick rush of air, the scary man is inches from Momma. She doesn't move.

"Momma?" I tug against her shirt.

The way she doesn't move to reassure me scares me more than anything else.

The man leans.

"That's my momma!" I kick him in the shins. "You're not allowed to kiss her!"

The man snarls at me with sharp teeth.

"Vampire!" I bolt for the house.

Inside the house I freeze, struggling to remember what Daddy said to do to fight vampires. There are too many rules about monsters and he promised they would never get us here. He lied.

"Georgie Porgie?" my brother calls as he comes through the back door. He must've escaped and is going to save me.

"Tyler! Vampires!"

Blood streams down my brother's body. He opens his mouth in a grin, revealing sharp, pointed teeth like I've never seen before.

Voices scream out warnings to run. Momma told me not to fear the voices. She can hear them too. It's her superpower. She says I'm just like her and will be a proper spirit guide. I don't always hear them. They always get louder when I get upset.

"Oh no! You're a vampire!" I stumble backwards, my eyes going as wide as saucers.

"You know you're not supposed to call people names. The beating of your heart sounds delicious." He licks his lips. "Come here!" He rushes forward with bared teeth.

I shriek and run.

He's faster than me. Tyler's hands grasp my arm, jerking me back to him. He sinks his teeth into my shoulder. It hurts bad enough I wet myself.

I hit him and run again. Over and over. I race from room to room unable to find a safe place to hide from him. His bites hurt worse than breaking my arm when I leaped off the swing. I flee into my bedroom, hoping to shut the door.

Tyler plows through my feeble attempts, sending me sprawling.

"Awe, Georgie Porgie, I want to play with you." He leaps on me like a cat with his favorite toy.

"No! Stop! Ow! Ty! You're hurting me!" I kick and punch with all my might to no avail. Blood flows from my shoulders, my arms, my legs. It's hot and sticky. Fatigue settles in. It's no use. I can't lift my arms to fight anymore.

He laughs louder all while nipping and scratching me. Then licking at the blood.

I scream and cry harder. Teeth. My brother's bloody teeth are all I see as he sinks them into my arms and legs.

And he stops. His head swivels toward the door.

Daddy, my savior, barrels in and freezes. His booming voice chants like the Father at church. His deep sing-song voice with the words I don't understand breaks with sorrow. He darts forward and kicks Tyler off of me.

Tyler snarls like a dog and crouches on the other side of the room.

Daddy places his foot against my butt and pushes me into the nearby closet.

I curl into a ball and wail in the dark for my Momma.

******

The hospital room returns Pinched faces of doctors and nurses stare down at me.

Wanting to escape their scrutiny, I turn my head away. "Daddy," I hiccup, and ugly cry as I struggle to sit up.

"He's right outside, sweetie," the nurse says.

Nathaniel's arms wrap around me.

I'm sorry, Georgina.

The shelter of Nathaniel holding me helps to calm my grieving heart. I can't take much more of this. My entire life is a lie. My brother tried to murder me. Vampires are real. My father saved my life. I'm married to a sex demon.

The doctors and nurses leave.

They're replaced by my father.

My lip quivers, and the waterworks start again. The voices whisper louder, creating an overload of noise in my head. All I can say to him is, "Ty."

Without hesitation my father rushes to me and pulls me into his arms. He doesn't say a single word, as he holds me.

I sob against his chest and cling to him for dear life. My whole life I thought he hated me, and that my brother and mother's deaths were my fault.

After several minutes of his tender embrace, I reduce from sobbing to jagged breaths.

He eases from my side and takes his seat again, keeping my hand in his. "I love you. Always have. When I sent you to London, I thought you were still in danger. I had to make certain commitments that I could not do while you were here without…" His voice falters, "your mother. I sent you to the one place I knew you would be safe. As soon as I was done with my commitments, I brought you home. I never once wanted you to suffer."

My eyes are sore from crying. "What commitments? Stop

holding back. No more secrets."

"To protect you and give you your life back, I stopped being a hunter."

Memories flutter to the surface. Tyler and he training together. My mother laughs as I try to mimic them. My brother was only three years older than me. All of them jumble together. My head pounds from the effort of trying to keep track of them.

Relax. We can work through them together.

It's too much. I can't do this.

Yes, you can. You're amazing. You're stronger than any person I've ever met.

Where are those voices coming from?

I don't know, they're...

They're what?

Dead.

As are you.

No, I am not. I have much to tell you. This is not the time. Your father needs your attention.

He doesn't need anything from me.

Georgina, please do not make me force you.

You wouldn't?

You need to focus on your father before he calls the doctor back in.

I blink, turning my attention back on my father.

His stony expression prevents me from reading his emotions.

"I'm sorry, Daddy, what did you say?" I guess that he asked me a question, and I didn't respond because I was talking to Nathaniel.

"I didn't say anything." He grimaces as he stares at me, like he's peeking into my soul.

I look down and fidget with the bedsheets, not wanting him to see my deep dark secret of Nathaniel. "Oh. Sorry. I'm exhausted," I mumble, hoping it deters him from asking any further questions.

His hand rests on my knee as he stands up. "Get some rest. I will see you in the morning."

"Okay," I chew against my lip as I watch him walk to the door. "Daddy, I love you."

He stops and looks over his shoulder at me. The smile that forms on his face makes my heart sing. "I love you too, baby girl."

CHAPTER TWENTY-FOUR

Locked in a Tower

March 15, 2019

The hollow, empty feeling, like a missing puzzle piece, is replaced by a minefield of trauma. Vampires are real. I shouldn't be surprised by this notion, considering I have been having a relationship with the voice in my head for months. My father made a deal with a fae to 'fix' me. I fear whatever that fix may have been undone with the amount of voices in my head.

Nathaniel's presence overshadows the voices. Despite his silence all morning, his excitement bubbles like a pot of water ready to flow over the rim.

I draw another heavy breath as I stare out the window, unwilling to engage with him. My anger trumps my need for his affection.

My father doesn't try to strike up a conversation since we got in the car. Even in the hospital he said maybe two words as he handed me a duffle bag with stuff from my apartment in it.

His silence is par for the course. One confession when he thought I might die, does not forgive a lifetime of deceit. I'm his fucking daughter. He should have told me sooner. Guilt replaces bitter resentment. I wouldn't have believed him had he told me before Nathaniel. I still don't believe he needed to send me away. How are we going to repair this relationship?

We pull up to the gate of my father's home, and he enters the code. The massive iron cage bars slide aside, and we ease up the drive. Our homecoming is more akin to entering a prison than my childhood home.

In front of our house sits a black Mercedes with dark tinted windows. I glance at it as we pass by to park in the garage.

"Go inside and do not leave" He's staring at the Mercedes while barking commands at me.

"Are you leaving?" Fear of being left alone in his home pitches my question higher than I mean to.

He doesn't even give me the courtesy of looking me in the eye when he snaps, "I said go inside and don't leave."

I cross my arms and stomp my foot.

This draws his attention to me and our staring contest affords me the first decent look at my father. His shirt's disheveled. Days old stubble on his face reveals the silver growing in his otherwise black hair. Dark circles accent his eyes, giving him a weary, battle-worn appearance.

I exaggerate exhaling as the desire to fight with him fizzles out. "Fine," I grumble and storm into the house.

You should be kinder to your father.

I didn't ask for your opinion.

He loves you, Georgina.

His love is based on lies. Lies he's told me my whole life.

To protect you.

Again, I didn't ask your opinion.

I pause in the doorway of my room. My screams from that evening echo in my mind like a horror movie's eerie warning music. I push back the tidal wave of emotions my father never allowed me to process and walk inside.

The bed is soft and welcoming as I flop on it.

An urgency rings in the cacophony of voices my father's confession unlocked.

How am I supposed to deal with all this when the person who knew how to is gone? How could my father do this to me? I roll onto my side and curl up, resentment stacking a lead weight in the pit of my stomach.

"Go away," I growl as I bury my face into the pillow I hug.

Nathaniel's gentle hand rests on my hip as the pressure of his body spoons mine.

I want to tell him off and shove him away. My pathetic need to have his attention causes me to hold my tongue.

Minutes tick by and the voices dissipate.

I remembered.

"I don't want to talk to you right now."

I understand. This cannot wait. Do you remember Raven's warnings?

I snort. He knows what I know, why ask me such a stupid question?

We have consummated.

His ominous tone stretches my emotional rubber band tighter, threatening to snap it clean apart. How was that even possible? Did I finger myself until I broke my hymen? There was blood on my hands. As gross as that thought is, the memory of his lips against mine and his cock filling me brings a blush to my cheek.

No! Stop!

The voices scream.

I flinch and cover my ears.

His arms wrap tighter around me.

I close my eyes tight, refusing to face this problem. It will all go away if I can't see it. No more feelings, or desires. I will curl up and stay in this ball forever.

I enlisted in the Tennessee Volunteer Army the night I announced my intentions to marry. You remind me of her, sweet and smart with a fiery temper. I should have married her before I left. Her father was having none of it. That's why I joined up. I wanted to prove to him I had what it took to marry his daughter.

Nathaniel keeps his tone low and even as he holds me close.

I thought we were going to be fighting the Rebs. I was mistaken. Our entire march to the sea was one shit show after another. Sherman spearheaded open warfare against not only the Rebels but the creatures of the night that were using them as pawns as well.

"Creatures of the night?"

Horrific monsters like the vampire that killed your family. I can't even begin to imagine the thousands of dollars' worth of Sterling silverware we melted over the course of that trip. We needed the metal to coat our musket balls to kill the creatures.

My shoulders relax and I lower my hands, the voices return to an irritating whispering.

Nathaniel presses on.

We tracked them clear across the South. It led us to Savannah, to Haven Hill. My unit was dispatched to scout the place and gather as much information as we could. We had every intention to slip in and slip out unseen. It was not to be.

We were waylaid by a group of women with a broken wagon. Their allure was beyond anything I had seen before or since. We didn't stand a chance as they invited us to join them at the main house as thanks for assisting them.

Even with my returned memories, what happened inside the house is hard to recall. All I have are flashes of myself in the carnal embrace of a woman who was not my fiancé.

Guilt rips at my insides as his inability to remain faithful torments him.

I am no better than your Richard, in the end. Just another cheating man. Maybe her father was correct in denying her hand to me. Georgie, life is short. You can make amends and talk to those you still care for.

"What do you mean?"

I mean you should reach out to her. As much as I want you all to myself, I know your heart. Do not push away those you love. You died. There may not be a tomorrow for you.

Despair threatens to paralyze me, even with his gentle nudging to move. I have been such a coward when it comes to Gracey. A fool chasing after a man who offered me nothing but regret. I ease up and Nathaniel's hand rests at the small of my back. What do I say to her? What will I do if she doesn't feel the same?

I will be with you no matter what.

Before I chicken out I push off the bed and rummage through my bag until I have my phone in hand. I expect it to be dead.

It turns on without issue.

I flip to messages and my finger hovers over Richard's name when I notice the unread messages from my father. My father doesn't text, especially not to me. I tap on my father's name to bring up the message history.

"Nathaniel? Did you send this message?"

I did.

My eyes fixate on the single four letter word sent to Dad from my phone the day I collapsed.

Help

"Oh Nathaniel," I bring my free hand up and cover my mouth as I cry. He saved my life with that text.

His arms wrap around me and he buries his face into the crook of my neck. He recounts what happened after I collapse. How he had to violate my rules and force my body to function at its most basic level.

While no one can see his embrace, I know he's there and I don't want him to leave. I need him. It isn't fair that we're trapped like this. He's not the only one I want in my life forever. Gracey is everything good in my life since I met her.

Need you. Locked in the tower. 911

omw

Before she arrives, I take a shower and change into the sweatshirt and leggings my father stuffed in the bag. Thinking about him rummaging through my apartment piles another stone of anxiety into the already large sack I'm carrying.

I tie my hair up into a messy bun and smother my face in moisturizer. My skin's paler than normal and my eyes are red from crying. The dark rings under them reminds me of the first time I tried to create a smokey eye effect and wound up looking more like a racoon.

"Georgie," Gracey calls.

"Up here," I shout as I exit the bathroom. Butterflies banish the lead weight in my stomach and I smooth my hands over my shirt.

She trots up the stairs, her overnight bag on her shoulder.

I barrel into her and pull her into the tightest hug I can muster.

"Whoa, hey. You tryin' to kill us?" She laughs as she clings to me and keeps us from tumbling down the stairs. Why are you moving around at all? You had a heart attack? You should be resting."

"I'm fine. I'm sorry. I should have told you sooner. I was just dumb and scared and not sure what was happening to me. I thought it was drugs. Then you didn't want me to, and I thought you hated me. And Richard, God stupid Richard. And then he texted him and we had this fight and… and... I woke up in the hospital. Then my dad, he... he told me about the vampires and I might die. I don't want to die. I want to live. I want to live with you. Gracey, I love you." I talk with my hands as much as my words as I flounder like a fish out of water in my word vomit.

Gracey's eyes are wide, her mouth open as if I had pressed pause on her. She's not responding to any of the things I said.

Fear propels me forward. I go for broke and I take hold of Gracey's jacket. I lean in and press my lips to hers, praying for the Disney magic of "true love's kiss".

Gracey's lips are sweet from her watermelon lip balm. My entire body melts as she pulls me closer, cups my face, and guides me into a kiss that makes my toes tingle. Our lips part as the tip of her tongue teases open my mouth.

I need her.

Richard's kisses were nothing like this. They had been chaste, or aggressive, leaving me dirty and used.

Gracey's lips are intoxicating, and the sparks are full of life. I moan into the kiss, clinging to her for dear life.

Her fingers dance along my neck and over my T-shirt, tickling me through my clothes. She dances me like a spicy tango towards my bedroom as she nibbles my skin while her fingers slip under my shirt.

When her hands cup my breasts and pinch my nipples, I whine.

"Gracey!"

"Yes, Georgie?" she purrs after releasing one breast to slide her hand into my pants.

Needy mewls are all I can manage as we stumble through my bedroom door.

She chuckles, her breath warm on my skin. "Tell me what you desire."

Her words rattle in my skull like a taunt, bringing my nightmare to life.

Nathaniel's cock thrusts into my ass, driving me forward into Gracey.

Her fingers work my clit harder.

Twisting to get free, I cry out and push Gracey. "Stop!"

Gracey leaps back like I struck her.

Nathaniel stops.

My breath comes too fast, and I can't stop the trembling that shakes me all over. Shame washes over me like a second shower, making my face burn.

Gracey stares at me, her body tense, her gaze critical.

"Gracey?" My voice is small and terrified.

She remains unmoving as she studies me, not answering my plea for her to say something.

I fear if I blink first, I will lose the only person in this world who loves me.

The bedroom grows cold as her expression darkens.

I turn away and sink to the ground. There is no-one left to love me.

A heavy ringing in my ears drowns out any sound. I was stupid to believe Nathaniel's encouragement. I'm pathetic and no one could love me. Now Gracey stares at me like I'm last night's garbage. I wish I had died.

Is that what you desire? An intoxicating feminine voice whispers in my head.

Stars burst before my eyes. A sharp sting radiates in my cheek.

Gracey's hands squeeze my shoulder, lines etch her skin as she stares down at me.

"Georgie! Answer me!" She shakes me hard enough the back of my skull bounces off the wall.

I yelp. Tears spring from my eyes. She jerks me forward, and her sobs echo mine.

"Don't scare me like that. I almost lost you again." Her voice hiccups between hitching cries..

"Wait… again?" I untangle from her clutches and pull back to look at her.

"Don't leave me alone," she whimpers and captures me again with a bear hug.

I cling to her like she's my life preserver in this sea of insanity. Sea salt and caramel scents engulf me as I bury my face in her shoulder.

She doesn't hate me. "Gracey, I-,"

"Georgie, it's okay." Her words are gentle and soothing. She eases back and brushes my damp hair from my face. "I think you need to hear what I have to say first."

No. No, she can't be keeping secrets from me. She was the one thing in my life that was supposed to be known and perfect.

Her smile is soft and comforting as she keeps her fingers in mine.

My eyes take in her exotic beauty, memorizing her as if this will be the last time I ever get to see her.

I remember the first time we met. I walked by while she was

buck-ass naked in the dorm showers. With the curtain wide open her flower tattoos and bare ass were on display for all to see. When she caught me checking her out, and trying to process why she would dye her hair down there blue, she teased me without mercy. After dying twice from embarrassment, we had spent the rest of the evening and into the night giggling and getting to know each other.

Gracey is always the confident and outgoing one of the two of us.

"I–" She swallows hard. "Georgie. I am a siren. And you are my soulmate".

Before I can register what she said, she continues. "I've known we were meant to be together since the first time I laid eyes on you. All you could see was Dick."

The words flow from her like a tsunami. "I never wanted to hurt you. I refused to force you to be with me. If I used my song to make you leave Dick, I could never live with myself. So I decided that being near you was enough. I've always envied the place that Richard had in your heart. Watching him put you through one awful thing after another tormented me, and I couldn't do anything to stop him. Oh, how I wanted to make him pay. But you loved him. And if it made you happy, I didn't want to take that from you."

My fists clench and I grind my teeth as the anger at yet another person I trust has been lying to me.

"Then you were done with him. I wanted to commiserate with you. I was elated at my chance to pick up the pieces and claim you for myself. I hate that I fixated on how I could make you mine." Tears stream down her cheeks as she takes my hands and clings to them as if I might try to run. "I know I should have said something sooner. Then you started to look at me. My heart rang like the church bells over a cathedral."

My brain struggles to catch up with her confession.

She mistakes my silence as her cue to continue. "Your aura changed. A parasite distorted your entire being."

A high-pitched squeal drowns out whatever else she says.

Parasite.

She knew. She knew and hid it from me. The entire time I was struggling, she pretended he wasn't there. I realize Gracey is silent, her lips caught between her teeth. Tears cling to her lashes as she awaits my response.

"Georgie…?" Her words are soft and childlike. Like she fears she might shatter me if she speaks louder.

A lump sits in the back of my throat. I could rage and scream at her for being like everyone else. For letting me suffer all this time alone, thinking I was crazy.

"How long?" I demand.

"How long?" She blinks, and she shakes her head like she has whiplash.

"How long have you known of Nathaniel?"

"I had my suspicions in Hilton Head. I didn't know for sure until it messed with you when I touched you today." She clings to my hands tighter.

"Why did you lie to me?"

"I wanted to tell you. While you were with Dick, I wouldn't do that to you. I couldn't shatter your happiness for my selfishness. I love you, Georgie. Always have, always will." She takes a deep breath. "Even if you want nothing to do with me. I will respect whatever choice you make."

Her hands tremble in mine.

This is the first time, ever, she looks small and vulnerable. She's always vibrant and wild, as untamable as the ocean. I have a choice to make, sitting on this harsh floor in my bedroom that ruined my life. Do I push her away and die, possessed by Nathaniel? Or do I fight for us?

CHAPTER TWENTY-FIVE

Tell Me No Lies

"Oh, Gracey, I could never hate you. I'm angry and hurt. One thing's for certain… I love you. The thought of you not being in my life, or hating me, crushes my very soul. I want, no, need, you in my life. The entire time I was with Richard, I knew you would always be by my side. That no matter how my day went, I could always confide in you. I never could do that with him." I shower her with kisses between sentences. I fling myself against her and hold on for dear life.

Gracey pets my back and kisses my forehead.

The lead weight of guilt and shame fades as I confess my love for her. Gracey is my anchor in this chaos.

"Feel better?"

"I'm scared Gracey," I sniffle against her.

"Of what?"

"Nathaniel," I whisper his name as if I could prevent him

hearing it.

"You gave the parasite a name?"

"Him."

"Him?"

"Not it. Him." I take a deep breath. "His name is Nathaniel. And as far as I can tell, he's as much a victim as I am."

"Really?" Gracey tilts her head and gives me the 'Bitch, please' look.

"Yes, really!" I whine. "I can talk to him, and the tale he tells is compelling. With his story fresh in my mind, I catch her up with what we know.

"Wait... you can talk with him?"

I laugh at her finding my ability to talk to him the surprising part of what I told her. Being able to tell someone and they not think I'm crazier than a lark allows me to relax. "You're a siren!"

"Yes, I am," she says, like she's talking to drunk Georgie.

"Well, can't you sing some kind of song and pull him out of my body? Like, lure him away? Back to Haven Hill or something?"

Her owl impersonation is on point. "Didn't you read the Odyssey in college? Y'know, the creatures that lure ships into the rocks to eat sailors? We don't go around performing exorcisms. I think you need a priest for that."

I giggle at her incredulous response. "Wouldn't that mean he has to leave a place to follow you?"

"Well, that's the mythology." She grouses. "We can manipulate emotions with our Songs. Some, of course, abuse this power and have lured men away for their own glee and gain. I've never heard of a siren luring a parasite, or dead person, anywhere. Usually, our prey has a pulse."

And it would kill you.

Nathaniel snaps.

Jealousy and anger flow through me like the dark side of the force as Nathaniel's feelings go unchecked.

I push up and pace in my room. I want to put space between the two of us to calm Nathaniel. My chest hurts again, and the last thing I need is a second heart attack in a week. The buzzing whisper of voices return, bringing a fresh throbbing to my temples.

Gracey flops on the bed, watching me like I'm the laser dot and she's a cat ready to pounce.

You want me gone that much?

The sadness in his voice brings tears to my eyes.

"No. Yes. Not gone. This isn't fair to either of us and–"

"What did he say?" Gracey hisses.

"He's upset that I want him out."

"Well, duh. He's a parasite, Georgie. Don't feed his wants."

"Look, he's part of me and ignoring him kills me faster!" The defensive anger as much from Nathaniel as it is me.

She flies off the bed and storms close. "Oh yeah? Well, listen here, Nathaniel. Georgina is meant for me. If she wants you gone, you're gone. A parasite like you is not going to take my mate from me." Her finger is in my face. Her eyes blaze bright violet.

The room tilts and the voices rise into a frenzied chorus of panic.

My heart races and thunders like a drum in my chest. "Gracey." I groan and clutch my chest with one hand and cover an ear with the other.

The stars burst in my eyes again.

What is it you desire?

The chorus taunts.

"Georgina!" Gracey's voice calls from a million miles away.

Georgina, listen to Gracey's voice. Don't listen to that —

You could have everything you ever wanted.

I close my eyes tight and sway in Gracey's arms.

"Georgie, I'm sorry. I love you. Please don't go. Please."

"I'm fine," I pant. "It's… this room. Bad memories." I lie and as she guides me downstairs.

Gracey gets me something to drink and leaves me alone on the couch.

The living room is quiet, other than the constant whispering chorus that follows me now.

"Want to talk about what happened up there?" She hands me the glass of water.

"No. I think I have to, though. You know how I always thought my dad hated me?"

"He doesn't hate you, Georgie."

"I know. Well, I think I do. Anyway. That's not the point. Apparently, my entire life is a lie and–" I swallow the taste of bile that welled up in the back of my throat. "Vampires killed my mom because my dad is a hunter."

The wheels spin a thousand miles a second as my neurons struggle to catch up. What if my father finds out she's a siren? Will he try to hurt her? "Wait… does that mean you will be in danger?"

Instead of her looking confused or worried, she looks down and fidgets with the hem of her shirt.

"Gracey?" Prickles of anger flare along my skin as I realize she's keeping another secret from me.

"I knew he was a hunter, that's all!" She snaps up her hands in defense.

"You… knew?!" My fists clench and I shout.

"He grilled me on my nature that first Christmas you brought me home from college." She shrinks.

"And he didn't do anything?"

"Well… Yes and no. He made it very clear that if I used my Song to influence you, he would make sure I regretted it." She drags her finger along her throat. "And that as long as I held to the Accord, he was duty bound to accept my presence."

"What accord?"

"The Accord." She scratches the back of her neck as she searches for the words. "It's like a binding agreement for those of us considered a xenospecies. The basic agreement is that if we don't try to hurt or hunt humans, the Council will help protect and shield us against their hatred. It's a way for us to all live together and be happy."

"Who is this Council, and do you think they could help me?"

"The Council is composed of all the major players, werewolves, vampires, and hunters. If the Accord holds and I'm in its territory, I don't have to be worried I'll get shanked in a dark alley by some misguided hunter who thinks I'm a scary beast."

The glint in her eyes makes me laugh with her at her morbid joke.

"I'm sorry."

"What? No! I'm the one that should be apologizing." Her hands flail as she waves off my apology. "I'm sorry. I should have told you this years ago."

"Starting this moment, I forgive you. I want us to be us, again."

"I… Thank you."

We fall into a comfortable silence, and I snuggle into her on the couch. Nathaniel seems to have disappeared again. Curiosity getting the better of me I ask, "Why did you pull away when we kissed?"

"Hmm? Oh. That." She blushes. "I… felt… it awaken." She shifts on the couch next to me. "I was so eager that you were coming to me, that I had let myself forget that parasite attached to you. Then it awoke, and it startled me. Besides, you screamed to stop! I'm not going to rape you."

"I'm not a parasite. I am her husband for Christ's sake!"

I cover my mouth before Nathaniel blurts something else. The last thing I want is for him to chase off Gracey.

No, Georgina. You let me talk with her. She may be your mate as she claims, but I am your husband. We are one. She will need to accept us both, or this will never work.

I lower my hand and chew against my lower lip before I nod.

"We are one, Sophia Grace. Georgina and I are bound in this body. To separate us is to kill Georgina." The voice is mine, calm and steady. The speech pattern and words are Nathaniel's.

My body is stiff and my hands are clenched in fists as Nathaniel controls my mouth without any effort. While he had used my body to text Richard in my sleep, he hadn't dominated me while awake before.

Gracey waits with a clenched jaw and a gleam in her eyes. She softens. Her voice is saccharine sweet when she speaks again. "We're going to play a game, parasite."

"My name's Nathaniel. I'm not a parasite. I'm a man…or I was." I huff. "Fine. We'll play your game, siren."

She starts with innocent questions. Asking him his favorite things.

His bemusement is muted as the overwhelming urge to prove himself fills me. He wants Gracey to like him.

With the baseline on his willingness to answer established, she turns her questions to our relationship. Asking his intentions for her mate. She taps her finger against her lips as she tries to trip him up with questions regarding things I love.

"Her favorite vacation place is Amsterdam," he beams.

My cheeks blush. I never told Nathaniel that was my favorite. I hadn't told Gracey either.

Her eyes narrow and she hums her response.

The questions kick up a notch as she grills him on the details of possessing me.

Nathaniel struggles and stutters in response, like streaming during spotty reception.

Pain radiates in my neck and I flex my fingers.

Gracey glances at my hand before looking me in the eye again. "One last question: Why did you butt in when we were getting frisky?"

Nathaniel hesitates in responding.

It's surreal having his emotions and knowing what he will say while being unable to move my mouth or body. I'm a floating blob in my body. Is this how is for him?

Yes, and no.

"Georgina's desire dictates my actions. The more aroused she becomes the more I seek to fulfill her every wish." He rubs the back of his neck as he struggles with guilt.

"Now that we have consummated, she is more susceptible–."

"Stop," I rasp as the vice grip on my chest ratchets to eleven and the void of Nathaniel leaving me causes me to whimper in pain.

Gracey's arms wrap around me.

The chorus of voices hiss and fade as my ears ring with the sweetest melody I have ever heard.

I curl into her and we rock as the pain subsides and I'm left panting against her.

"What is happening to you, Georgie?"

"I don't know. Raven said something about the Master and Nathaniel's growing stronger. The whole time you two were talking, it was like I was watching a movie, far away and wasn't in my body at all. If we talk about Haven Hill and what happened there, it hurts. Like he's being torn out of my chest level pain."

"Then how do we fix it?"

"I've tried researching everything I can think of. The library was useless. Even their occult section is full of nothing on possessions, or rituals. It's all the Kitchen Witch and crystal stuff." I scoot back on the couch, bringing my knees up to hug them to my chest and rest my chin on them. "Maybe this is how it's supposed to be."

"The fuck it is!" Gracey growls at me and shoots up off the couch like a rocket. "Come on. I know a place."

"My dad said to stay here."

"Yeah, well, he's not here and I'll be damned if I'm going to let you sit around and mope like this. If there's any kind of answer that can help you," she motions in a circle around me, "then this place will have it."

I chew against the inside of my mouth as I watch Gracey. I've never seen her this agitated. Her hand is offered, and she shifts her weight from foot to foot.

We have to try Georgina. It could let us all be together without me controlling you.

Nathaniel's hope surprises me. This is the first time I've heard him talk about being anything other than in my body.

When I slide my hand into Gracey's she squeals and pulls me into a tight hug.

"I should at least leave my dad a note, so he doesn't freak out."

CHAPTER TWENTY-SIX

Famous Last Words

The drive across town is uneventful. I'm on edge, expecting my phone to ring at any moment with Dad demanding I come home and rest. He must still not be home yet, which is surprising. My father doesn't like anyone to be in his home when he isn't there, even if that someone is his daughter. I wonder who waited for him in that car that he would abandon me again. I hope he's not in some kind of trouble. We may be weird with each other, but he's still my dad.

Gracey pulls into the parking lot of a run-down strip mall. The parking lot jars me like an old rickety roller coaster with all the potholes. She parks before a simple storefront with two neon signs. One reads The Bookstore and the other flashes 'Open'. Next to it, is a gyros place, then an insurance agent, followed by none other than 1-800-PSY-CHIK.

As soon as she stops the car, I hurry out of the passenger side.

Hope springs anew. The business card Raven left said The Bookstore.

It also said to ask for Khaylia.

"You know this place?" Gracey's doubtful expression that I would ever come to this side of town on my own leaves me feeling two inches tall.

"No, not really. It's… this crazy con artist left the card on my table when she came and did all this weird hoodoo voodoo to me."

Gracey turns to face me and grabs my shoulder to force me to look at her. "What do you mean hoodoo voodoo?"

The seriousness with which she asks that question makes me laugh. I right myself when she doesn't laugh with me.

"She called herself Madame Raven and put this blue goop that stung on my forehead. Then she brought out a crystal ball and I could see Nathaniel in it."

She's still not amused. She inspects my forehead then nods and marches me toward the glass door with the hours sign posted and a small, hand-written note that says, 'No Goblins Allowed'. The menagerie of incenses bombards my senses. Every way I turn, there are random crystals and tchotchke charms all over cluttered shelves. Countless pendants depicting Wiccan symbols hang from tiny display.

Gracey takes my hand and pulls me deeper into this tourist trap. We pass ominous and tall bookshelves, lined with everything from modern day kitchen witch books to old hand-bound books. Leather and paper scents mix with the heady incense. I revel in the smell only a good bookstore can have and blush when I hear Gracey chuckling next to me.

"Welcome to The Bookstore. Just ask if you need anything." The young man behind the counter doesn't stop what he's doing.

"Frances?" Billy Coeh's son working in a bookstore doesn't compute in my brain. Billy and his crew are all one wet T-shirt contest away from being illegal. He can't have a nerdy bookstore son.

"Miss Belmont?" He squeaks, turning as red as a tomato. He rubs his hands on his jeans and then through his dark curly hair. In contrast to Billy he's tall and slender with the softness of Shelley Coeh's face.

"It is you!" I chirp in delight as I walk over. "How are you? It's been, what, a couple of years?"

"Yes, ma'am." He bobs his head. "Not since you came over for that cookout my dad did for the construction guys."

"Oh, sorry." I motion to Gracey. "Gracey, this is Frances Coeh. Billy's eldest."

"Hey, Frances. Nice to meet you." She gives him one of her megawatt smiles.

I stifle a laugh at how his eyes widen and dance, trying to stay on her face.

"Um, yeah. Like I said, if you need help finding anything..."

"Will do!"

"He's cute" Gracey elbows me.

"Uh-huh, and his dad is scarier than mine."

We share a giggle and start to wander through the bookstore. The books are organized on the shelves in such a meticulous manner, making this more like a library than an occult bookstore.

"Where should we start?"

"Hrm, pretty sure there is a ritual section somewhere. I think the owner changes the layout all the time to keep people on their toes."

"Do you know the owner?"

"Not really, just in name. Anyone who's into this stuff for real knows her and knows she can get her hands on whatever you need."

"What's her name?"

"Khaylia Danisomething."

I freeze, an icy shiver running down my spine. "Excuse me, Gracey."

Hurrying back to the counter, "Frances, is Khaylia here?"

He looks up to meet my gaze and inspects me several seconds before answering, "No ma'am. She's out for the night."

He's lying.

How do you know?

His ears are turning red and he's starting to sweat.

"Frances, please. It's important." Pouting and sucking against my lower lip.

He scrunches his brow and looks toward the back of the store before meeting my gaze again. "She's not here… I'll tell her you want to talk to her. Leave me your number."

Why would he lie to me? Could I get back there before he could stop me and confront her? Would she do something awful to me? Like turn me into a toad or something. "Okay then." I retrieve a business card and hand it to him. "Please tell her it's urgent. Raven said I should talk to her."

Frances's eyebrows shoot straight up to his hairline. "I will, ma'am. I promise."

Leaving him to his work, I head back into the maze of bookshelves. I trail my fingers along the spines of the books. Lost in my thoughts, I bump into Gracey who stopped in front of a locked curio cabinet.

The edges of the books inside are frayed and their covers are faded.

We stand shoulder to shoulder as we stare at the books.

Gracey shrugs and moves on, continuing the hunt.

I'm frozen in place. My heart races. A shiver runs down my spine, and my skin crawls. The book commands my full attention.

"That one." I point at the nondescript book, bound in ruddy brown wrinkled leather. The pages have yellowed with age and appear to be bound by hand-sewn thread.

I never thought a book could sing. This one belts out an all-out rock ballad to me.

Georgina, I don't think this is the appropriate choice.

"What about that one?" Gracey comes back to me.

I can't take my eyes off the book, as if it will disappear when I blink.

Nathaniel, you sense it, don't you?

I can. Doesn't mean it's a good idea.

If it's connected, we have to get it.

No. That book is dangerous. The proprietor of this establishment should remove it from the shelf.

Nathaniel. No harm ever came from reading a book, and if it can help us, we should at least try.

"Georgie? What do you think of this book?" Gracey tugs my arm.

"It's linked."

"Linked? How?"

"It's singing to me. This book has something to do with this mess, and I need to read it."

"Um… no.

"What do you mean, 'no'?" I snap at her.

"These kinds of things can be dangerous, and if it wants you to read it, that's even worse. How can you be certain it will have anything to do with what we're dealing with?"

"You were the one who mentioned this idea. You were the one who said that if there was a chance of finding something to do with this curse, this would be the place to do it."

"I don't like the fact that on your first time here, you find 'the one book'. That's not normal."

"Really?" I growl. "You're going to tell me any of this is normal?" I puff up and cross my arms. "I'm tired of being an unwitting pawn in this universal bullshit, and if this Goddamn book can help then I am going to read the Goddamn book."

My anger breaks the staring spell. I turn on heel to storm back to the front of the store to get Frances and Gracey catches my arm.

"I'm sorry." She pauses. "I want to make sure we're as safe as we can be. Some of this stuff can be scary if we're not careful."

I wilt under her concern. "I want to find something, anything, that will help me… us, and I feel it in my bones. That book is crucial."

She relents.

We stand side by side as Frances rings us up.

"That'll be twelve-hundred-eighty-four and seventy-three cents, ma'am."

I blink. "Twelve hundred dollars? For a book?"

"Yes ma'am. That's what it came up as. These old books can be quite pricey."

I switch from the bank card I was fishing out of my wallet to the black American Express instead. I cradle the small plastic bag to my chest as we get back into the car.

Gracey fires it up and pops on the passenger light for me. "Let's see what it has to say."

My fingers tremble as I pull it out. The inexplicable warmth under my touch causes me to hesitate. The binding of the book doesn't feel like any material I have ever felt before. It's soft and pliable, like rabbit skin.

Georgina, this is an awful idea.

His words are in time with him locking me in place, keeping me from opening it.

"You promised. Never. Again." My muscles return to my control, and I take a couple of deep breaths to recenter.

The book fits open in my palms. I can't read what it says, and my heart sinks as I turn the pages. I hoped that it would be Latin or a Romance language, but the markings are foreign and illegible.

Tears threaten as frustration boils inside me. After all the posturing I had done regarding how important this book is, I hold useless gibberish.

Only if that is what you desire it to be.

The feminine voice whispers like a lover in my ear. I should fear whatever is talking to me. All I can think of is how much I want to read this book.

"You should close it." Gracey whimpers.

The words hold my gaze as they reshape and reform themselves into a variant of Latin I understand. I trail my nail along as I sound out words on the page.

Gracey reaches over and slams the book closed.

Ripped from my trance, I open my mouth to give Gracey what-for when I see she's trembling and pale.

"Georgie, you can read that?"

"I think so?" I try to put together what was happening. "I couldn't. Then… the script re-arranged itself, and I can make it out."

She flinches.

"Gracey?" Panic wells as the book pulses against my palm. The compulsion to open it and continue reading calls me.

She shakes her head no and turns, focusing on starting the car.

The horrible sense that I've hurt her causes me to shove the book back into the bag, drop it on the floorboard between my feet, and try to forget it exits the entire drive back to my dad's house. I'm expecting him to be there, waiting to catch me sneaking back in. When we discover he's still gone, I grow even more anxious. I was hoping we could ask him for help, or at least to translate as his Latin is much better than mine.

I set the book on the kitchen island, and we stare at it as if it were the monster book from Harry Potter and we wrestled it closed.

"What do we do now?" I ask Gracey.

She shakes her head and shrugs. "I'm a siren, not a witch. We don't all know everything about the Underworld."

"Should I try reading it again?"

"Whatever you were reading in the car made me sick to my stomach, like it was sucking my soul out of my skin."

Is there not a resource you could call upon to aid in this endeavor?

"No, Nathaniel, I don't have the number for-,"

Gracey looks at me like I lost my mind when I rush past her to the phone on the kitchen wall. I dial 1-800-PSY-CHIK.

"You're a damn fool, Belmont." Madame Raven's voice comes through the speaker after one ring. "You should wrap that book in blessed linens, holy water, and ash oil. Bury it beneath the oak tree in your backyard and forget it ever existed."

She sighs and continues. "The boy will kill ya if you do nothing. I don't know where you got that book, and I don't wanna know."

Then her words make no sense, like she's talking to someone else. "Damn, now I will need to talk to Lia. That's beside the point. If you must re-. Who the hell do I think I'm talking to? Of course you're going to read it."

I wait for her to turn her attention back to me, having experienced her weird conversation quirks before.

"Focus on specific words, or a few two to three-word phrases. Do not read entire sentences and do not read it aloud. You will find what you need. I warn you Georgina Belmont: You will also find extreme danger. I still say you should bury the damn book out back and make peace with the parasite. May the spirits guide you in your efforts."

She hangs up.

"What did she say?"

"That we should bury the book and to not read it out loud."

"There is a dark aura around that book, Georgie, like the one hovering around you."

"Wait, what?" I study her face, trying to decipher what she means. I should forget this book and find another way to save myself. The more I resist the urge, the stronger I sense the answer waits for me within its pages.

Then why do you hesitate?

Nathaniel's question gets me to pause. I take a deep breath and hold it for a three-count. I let the air out as I turn back to the book.

"Gracey, Nathaniel, I know this is risky, even borders on stupid. It's a matter of time before Nathaniel can't massage my heart to get it to restart." My voice trembles as I face my mortality.

"Wait, what!?" Gracey swoops around the island and twirls

me to face her. "What do you mean Nathaniel massaged your heart to keep you alive."

"Exactly what it sounds like. The only reason I survived was because of Nathaniel." I grit my teeth and straighten up to look her in the eyes. "He is killing me, Gracey. Maybe not today, maybe not tomorrow. While we are of one body, it can't handle both of us in it."

I take her hands and entwine my fingers through hers. "If this book can help me end this madness, I have to try." I take one more deep breath to steel my resolve. "Will you help me?" Fear twists my gut into knots. If Gracey walks out on me, I won't survive.

She collapses under the weight of my gaze. "Fine. I'll always help you, Georgie." We turn back to where the book lies unassumingly. "So, what do we need to do?"

CHAPTER TWENTY-SEVEN

Not on the New Floors

Touching the book a second time does not improve Gracey's disposition. The longer we look through it, the worse she reacts. Her skin pales, which I didn't even think possible, and she breaks out in a sweat. She sticks with me until she rushes to the nearest bathroom where she vomits.

I found the ritual I think will free Nathaniel's soul. My eyes dart across the page, failing to follow all the directions Raven gave me.

I slam the book closed, startling myself.

"Stop taking over my body!" I growl at Nathaniel.

Nothing good will ever come from reading this. I will protect you first and foremost, no matter the cost.

I open my mouth to protest and Gracey heaves again. If reading this book makes her violently ill, how can I ask her to help me with this? Is the book doing something to her that it isn't doing to me? I take a step toward the door to go help Gracey.

The book calls to me and I turn back. The sweet song fills me with energy and excitement.

Danger!

The voices crescendo in warning.

Nathaniel's hands on my shoulders turn me to the door then vanishes.

I force myself to ignore the call and leave the kitchen to find Gracey on her knees, crying over the toilet.

Gracey's the strong one. She's the one who wets the washcloth and holds my hair while dabbing my neck to comfort me when I party too hard. This isn't partying. Both times I touched that book she suffered.

Fear coats my stomach with lead as I run the washcloth under cold water, gather up her hair, and dab her neck to soothe her.

"We should bury the book." I say after she calms down.

"What? Why?"

"Because I want to read every single word on the page. It's like a drug. The more I read, the better I feel. Like I could have whatever I want..." My lip trembles as I realize that I'm irritated that I can't be in the kitchen reading the book. "Because it hurts you. You never get sick. Or shake. Or fear anything. In the last few hours, I have seen all that from you, Gracey. You said we're mates. Mates don't hurt each other."

Gracey scoots back and leans against the wall. She takes my hand and tugs.

I sit next to her.

"You always have been the goodie two-shoes." She nudges me. "Us finding this book wasn't a coincidence. You deserve to live, Georgie. If I have to puke my brains out all over your place for that to happen, then so be it. Do you think there is anything in the book that can actually help?"

I don't look at Gracey, not wanting her to see that I believe the book can solve all our problems. I will free Nathaniel, and the three of us can live happily ever after.

Is the book the answer, or am I being manipulated? What does it mean to free Nathaniel's soul? He doesn't believe he's dead. How can he be alive after all this time? If Gracey gets sick with me only reading the book, what happens if we perform the ritual?

Swallowing hard, I fight back tears. I don't know what to do. A mistake could be fatal. I refuse to put Gracey in that kind of danger. I'm going to die either way. If I can save her then it doesn't matter.

I lower my head as guilt fills me. Nathaniel is nothing but supportive. He makes me feel smart and beautiful. He holds me close. Despite our rocky start and forced proximity, he is more of a lover than Richard ever was. How can I consider doing this to him? What if this means he will be killed? Or worse?

Our life is on the line, regardless. As much as I hate to admit this, that book is key to our survival.

What if it kills you?

If my death means you live, then I will pay that price a thousand times over.

What if you go to Hell, or somewhere worse?

It would be the least I deserve for what I have put you and the other brides through.

Nathaniel! Don't say that. They cursed you into this existence. You are a victim as much as I am.

His easy-going chuckle rings in my ears.

"Georgie..." Gracey nudges me.

"The book can help." I push up and offer her a hand to help

her stand. "I have a plan."

"That's my girl!" She crows as she follows me out of the bathroom.

We head upstairs and I rummage through my room.

"He, will you check in my closet for a black back with a gold zipper. It has a bunch of stuff I had in my dorm room that can help us."

Okay, she'll go in the closet. The door opens out. I'll shut the door and block it with a chair. Then she'll be safe and we can do this.

Crap, I have to stay against the door. How will I reach the chair?

"Georgie," Gracey's facing me, her hands on her hips.

"Yeah?" I play innocent.

"What are you plotting?"

"Nothing," I squeak.

"Georgina Belmont. We damn well know, I have read you like a book since the first day we met. You're up to something. Spill the beans!" She brandishes a finger at me as she exits the closet.

Busted.

Nathaniel's laughing.

I hang my head, the flaming heat of embarrassment washing over me.

"The funny thing about being mates," Gracey coos as she comes close and Eskimo kisses me, "You know everything."

"Really?"

"No, silly goose, it's why I'm asking. Remind me to never ask you to bury the body. We'd both end up in prison."

I roll my eyes and laugh. The moment of brevity helps ease my anxiety.

"I was going to lock you in the closet and perform the ritual, and save the day," I huff at being thwarted.

"No, Georgie." Gracey stops smiling. "We are in this together. I go where you go."

"But-."

"No buts. Quit fucking around tell me how to help you."

******

The gravel crunches under the tires sounding like bones crushing as we approach the house. There's no light. Causing the massive plantation house looming in the distance to be hard to see. This house is massive and beautiful during the day, even in its dilapidated state. With the scaffolding reflecting the headlights, I get the impression of a beast caged in the shadows tonight.

The voices grow in number, turning from an annoying, perpetual whisper to a dull roar, like I'm standing in the center of a gladiator stadium. Their incessant chanting warning of danger.

Nathaniel's hands rest on my shoulders and the weight is like he's sitting behind me and reaching over the seat. His emotions pound against mine like the tide rolling in.

Any thoughts I had of concentrating were foolish.

Gracey parks in front of the steps and kills the engine, throwing us into darkness.

My eyes are drawn to the second story and to the bedroom where this all began and a shudder rips through me. The tentacles holding me in place, a massive cock shoving down my throat. My jaw aches from clenching it tight and my fists curl around the seatbelt as if it could shield me from the house.

"You okay over there?"

"No," I confess.

Her hand rests on my knee.

I close my eyes and take slow, deep breaths. The warmth radiating from her touch banishes the slimy tentacles. It silences the roaring voices Coupled with Nathaniel's firm embrace, the cloud of fear dissipates.

"Okay, we go into the house, set up the circle as described and read from the book. Nothing more, nothing less." I run through the steps that I committed to memory, trying to psych myself up.

"You're sure we have to do this while it's dark? Wouldn't it be better to come back during the day?"

"It requires to be performed during the witching hour."

"Then I guess we better hurry." She points at the glowing readout on the dash of the car.

"We have plenty of time, a full thirty minutes." I try to joke, and my voice cracks from fear.

Dressed like we're ready for a pajama party, we force ourselves from the safety of the car and gather the plethora of items to haul inside. The book was explicit regarding every detail, including having to wear natural fibered clothing. All I could find in my childhood bedroom were cotton shirts and shorts.

Gracey unlocks the door with my code. The massive double doors swing inward, their old hinges groaning under the weight of the oak.

With no HVAC system installed, the inside of this massive house is stuffy and hot, causing our cotton shirts to soak against our skin. I don't know how Billy and his crew work in these conditions.

The interior is coming along. No doubt the main floor looks amazing hidden under the gray safety paper. Billy's crew always does perfect work for me.

"Ready, you two?"

"Y'know, you sound like a mad woman?"

She's not wrong. I'm going mad.

Nathaniel says nothing. The firm squeeze on my shoulder lets me know he's still present.

We slip out of our shoes and step into the foyer.

The light won't turn on.

I lie to myself that Billy turned the power off during the night to conserve cost.

Gracey walks around the perimeter and places camping lanterns. Within minutes, LED light floods throughout the main room.

The air is thicker and heavier with the doors closed, like someone threw a wet blanket over the entire house, making it harder to breathe.

My hands tremble as I fish out the book.

It's okay, Georgie. I will protect you; I swear.

I close my eyes and take a deep breath to calm my racing heart. This is insane. We're insane. Who in their right mind would read ancient rituals out of a book they just found?

Despite my rational brain's resistance, my instincts tell me this is the only way. I flip it open to my bookmark and skim the shifting markings again. My college love of Latin pays off tonight as the scribbles morph into legible words.

"First, I need to draw the circle."

I rustle through my purse until I pull out the cheap lipstick I bought at the store. I stare down at the paper covering the floor. "Gracey, come help me peel this back. The circle must be on the floor, not the paper."

It hurts my soul to blemish such stunning work. Billy and his crew had redone the porcelain and marble and my hand hovers over the glistening tile for a heartbeat.

He'll understand.

"I'll buy you new tiles," I murmur in apology to the floor before smearing the lipstick on it. Going slow while holding the book in one hand, I move around the floor, drawing the circle in place.

"Then we draw a star."

"Pentagram," Gracey snaps at me, lingering near the wall. "You're drawing a pentacle Georgie. A pentagram inside a circle is called a pentacle." There's an edge in her voice.

I finish the pentagram and frown at her. "Are you okay?"

"Yup. Just want you to know what you're doing. This is witchcraft, Georgina. Are you sure this is the one? This isn't a paint by numbers kind of thing. You need to be absolutely certain." She's shaking like a leaf and breathing through her mouth.

"I…I'm sure." I'm not. The weird nagging feeling that we'll never get another chance pushes me to keep going. "We need to put the bowls at the five points and burn them."

Five copper bowls are placed on the points and filled with the herbs.

They flare to life as I touch each one with the long match, dancing like little goblins around the circle. The ease with which they light makes me feel like the house wants us to succeed and is helping us.

"You have your part to read?"

"Still sure I need to read this?"

"According to the notes, I need a congregation, and you're the only one I got."

We echo each other with nervous laughs.

"Here goes nothing." I sink to my knees in the center and set the book in front of me. "I love you Gracey." I blurt.

Her head snaps up, and she meets my gaze. "I love you too, you dork. Let's get this over with and then we can have all the hot steamy make-up sex."

My cheeks burn hot and I genuinely laugh.

You can do this, Georgina. Slow and steady.

I nod to Nathaniel and begin reciting. The words sound absurd to my ears, and are a kick to the gut as the first harsh consonants slip past my lips.

The air in the house stirs. The walls and floors creak like someone cracking their knuckles.

I force myself to focus on my part and continue chanting.

Lost in the enthralling draw of the book, Gracey's chorus fades.

As I come to the end of the chant, the house groans, and the flames in the cauldron whip like tiny minions eager to invite their leader to the party.

I pause.

The spell starts over and keeps flowing from my mouth. A scream lingers in my throat, replaced by the violent words.

My hands remain planted on the book and my ass lifts into the air and my knees skid apart like a bitch in heat. I told my body to stand up and to throw the book.

The spell's chant rings louder and louder, no matter what I do.

The walls shudder as if they mock me with laughter.

Dark tendrils ripple across the floor slithering along my sweat-soaked skin, slithering under my clothes to slime their way over every inch of me.

Georgina!

Sultry feminine laughter drowns out Nathaniel's panicked

shout.

You have done well, vessel. Cum for me.

Tears roll down my cheeks like tiny waterfalls.

A thick tentacle slaps against my pussy. It's sharp and stings before gliding along my lips to force its way in.

More coil around my breasts until my nipples are pinched and tugged into tight buds.

A smooth head trails along my ass until it thrusts into my clenched hole.

My chanting is muffled by the massive cock stuffing my mouth, but I don't stop.

Shame flames my skin hot as my eyes close.

Gracey's throaty moan makes my clit throb in needy frustration.

In my heart, I hate that she is forced into this abuse. My body doesn't care and my arousal skyrockets at the thought of her joining me in it.

Good vessel, that's right. Give in to your desire.

Her praise fills me with a sense of belonging. I need her affection. I want to please her. Only her. She is my Master and I must give her everything.

Like the whore I am, I moan as I climax.

CHAPTER TWENTY-EIGHT

Avon Calling

"Wake up, damn it!" Raven slams her fist into the small walk-up's door. "I know you're in there, Lia! Open up! It's an emergency!"

"That damn fool girl is going to get herself killed." The spirits around her are screaming into the void. She tries to focus on waking the one person who can help and ignoring their frantic pleas to help Georgina.

"I know she's in trouble, you damn banshees! Shut it already!" She shouts at the spirits.

"If you wanted me to shut it, why the hell did you pound on my door?" Khaylia Danakar rolls her eyes as she appears in the doorway, a glass half-full of whiskey and ice in hand.

"There's no time. Come! Come!" Raven grabs her hand and jerks her towards the car.

"Like hell I am!" She pops her wrist out of Raven's grip and bounces back a step. "Tell me what're you worked up for already, woman!"

"I don't have time for this. The Belmont girl is a damned fool, that's what! And if we don't get a move on it, we'll be too late."

Khaylia inhales and studies Raven like she threw shit at her before she throws back the remains of her whiskey and follows. "You owe me for this." She locks up behind her before sliding into the passenger seat of the little blue Geo Metro.

When Raven turns the key, the vehicle sputters and refuses to start.

"I know you don't want to go there," she snaps at the dash. "I don't care where you want to go. They need us, so we go."

The little car chokes to life.

"You gonna tell me what the fuck is going on here?" Khaylia's accent grows thicker with her temper.

She never explains why she slips into a Cajun accent when she loses control. She's an enigma, even to the spirits. Someone keeps her identity hidden, but that doesn't stop Raven from using her abilities to help the spirits or people like Georgina.

"The Belmont girl got that accursed book from you. She plans on reading it. And if we don't hurry, she'll awaken the House." she death grips the steering wheel.

The car whines its protests as she presses it to over a hundred miles per hour.

"Fuck dat noise? I didn't give no book to no baby hunter. You're talkin' out your ass." Khaylia spits back. "You fuckin' think I have a death wish? Plus, that damn house been sleepin' for years. You said the renovations was nothin' to worry about."

"I was mistaken."

"What do you mean, mistaken? You're never wrong," her voice rises an octave.

Raven cuts her a hard glance. "No, I can be mistaken. I don't like when it happens." She whips her head around to the driver-side door. "I know I have to hurry! Hush while I focus on driving. I was hopin' the girl and the spirit would resolve themselves peacefully. Instead, the damn boy fell in love. We both know that if there is any power in this mortal realm that can alter fate, it's love."

"I still don't see what any of this has to do with me, or why you think I gave her a book." she huffs in the passenger seat.

"She got the key from your bookstore."

"My bookstore! I don't carry that Fae bullshit on the public shelves! Nor do I have anything even remotely looking like a key to an ancient evil prison."

"What's done is done. I'm not powerful enough to save the girl from this monster. The best I can do is get you an opening."

Khaylia sputters. "Oh, Hell No! I am not shadow walking to rescue some dumb bimbo from a fucking elder God! Nope! No fucking way. Those elder fucks aren't to be trifled with. Especially on the Ides of March!"

"If you don't do this, she will complete what was stopped and open the gates."

"Shit. Then why ain't you goin' faster?" Khaylia hates it when the world turns and burns on her shoulders. She was supposed to be done with this bullshit. Raven knows exactly what buttons to push to get to her cave and that pisses her off even more.

The spirits settle into tense silence as they race to the plantation. Within minutes, they're banking off the highway and careening around the corner to the long drive.

Khaylia narrows her eyes as they pull up next to a massive pickup truck. The headlights from the compact car illuminate a mountain of a man lifting himself off the ground. A silent string of profanity in some long-dead language burns off her tongue as the man staggers.

"Billy Coeh, what in the Nine Hells are you doing here?" Khaylia pops out of the passenger side of the car before it comes to a stop.

"Ms. Danakar?" The massive Alpha of the Coeh pack whirls around. "And Madame Raven? Oh, thank the Goddess. The boys told me there was activity at the house. When I got here, I tried to get into the place. The doors wouldn't open, so I threw my shoulder into it. The damn thing punted me. I tried again, and I'll be damned if a tentacle didn't try to choke the life outta me. Somethin' happened then and that damn house threw me like a damn tennis ball." His growl sends shivers up their spines.

"Of course it did, Alpha." Raven marches past him and strides toward the house. "The house is awakening, and she will never let you interfere."

"What!?" Billy's roar of a shout causes Khaylia to wince.

"Hush, man. We're here to help. Stop your yapping and heel. I need to borrow some of that brute strength of yours if you want to save the girl."

Billy's pauses and flits his gaze between the women. Any other people in Savannah dare to tell him to heel like a dog would lose their head. His chest rises and falls as he struggles to rein in the triggering reaction to being insulted. He was supposed to keep Georgina safe from all this, helping her father honor his half of the fae bargain. Ripping off heads will have to wait. "Whatever you need."

Khaylia gives him an approving smile. "You must like the girl to offer yourself without first asking what I intend to do."

"Don't test me, mage." Billy snarls as she approaches. "Franky trusts you. Which means I'm willing to believe that you're here to help. Don't make me regret that."

Khaylia takes a deep breath to prevent herself from picking a fight with an Alpha werewolf is as dumb as two girls reading from an Elder God's book of spells. "Keep your eyes down. Don't talk to the voices. Hold on tight."

"Hold on tigh-?" Billy repeats.

The landscape shimmers and shifts. Dark tendrils of smoke rise from the ground and disappear into the star-laden void above. An omnipresent glow shimmers around them. The only connection out of the in-between is Billy Coeh. He is her anchor, and the beacon to allow Khaylia to traverse the shadow realm onto other plains.

She stretches and eases from him. The phoenix of chaos always burns bright in the Shadow Realm, no matter how much energy she possesses. She faces away from Billy, staring down the true form of the plantation before daring to storm in. This is dangerous even when planned and secured with multiple anchors. One wrong step and not only will she perish, but Billy's soul will be trapped in the in-between.

"Ms. Danakar?" Billy's voice echoes, like he calls to her in a dream. He takes a step forward and Khaylia whirls around to face him. "I fucking told you to stay put!"

"No, ma'am, you didn't. You said, keep your head down, don't look at anything and hold on tight. How the fuck am I gonna hold you iffn you walk away?"

Khaylia frowns. She shouldn't be doing this tonight. How many glasses of whiskey did she have before Raven showed up? She closes her eyes and centers. This is too critical to be this sloppy.

"You're my anchor, Alpha Coeh. You need to stay in that spot. No matter what you hear. Do not move. Do not engage. I will need all your strength if we're going to succeed at all. Is that understood?"

He nods. He's an all-powerful Alpha. He should be the one to save the girls.

Satisfied he is not going to further endanger them, she turns to face where the house was.

The mansion's facade fades into a writhing sea of tentacles. Large, small, and massive vines wrap and layer upon each other to create a facsimile of a house.

Madame stands before the front door, her true aura bold and beautiful. Gone are her drab pajamas, and instead a regal red gown hugs every delicate curve of her body. The skirts billow around her in the tainted wind. A train of flower petals flow from her shoulders.

"Behave," Raven commands.

The singular word rips across the starry sky like a biting whip.

Khaylia rushes forward as the tendrils recoil from Raven and slips inside to a different dimension. Where wall sconces and wainscotting hung, now are phallic sculptures and grinding bodies. The floors are carpeted with bodies writhing in the throes of ecstasy. Rotting flesh of tortured souls who succumbed to this Elder God's power.

Tentacles slither and writhe, taking the shape of cocks as they penetrate any willing hole offered to them. The stench of stale sex mixes with death and burns my nostrils..

She pushes deeper in and her foot slips off the slick breasts of some writhing, faceless woman beneath her. "I. Fucking. Hate. It. Here."

Then leave.

The booming feminine voice ricochets off the sex walls and causes Khaylia to wince. The flames of her aura shudder in disgust.

Her eyes scour the mass of erotic flesh until she finds, high upon a dais of women in the throes of orgasm, a shapely woman form shrouded in the ethereal tendrils of darkness. Where her eyes should be galaxies swirl.

"Make me," Khaylia snorts like a taunting child. Her flames flare as she rushes forward. Elder Gods can read people's minds. Khaylia moves without thought, preventing the monster from getting a lock on her.

The bodies held in the throes of ecstasy scream as their skin burns and disintegrates under Khaylia's essence. Tentacles and worshipers alike skitter away like roaches when the light flicks on, cutting a clear path to the Elder.

At her feet is a single woman on her hands and knees. Tentacles pound and penetrate her body as they hold her in place on all fours.

Her body convulses and trembles as she moans.

Insolent whelp.

A thunderous wave of power thunders through the house.

The burned flesh of a soul lost to lust touches Khaylia, and wanton lust rips through her like lightning. Her aura burns hotter with passion. She pants, struggling to not succumb to the need to find the nearest pole and ride it into eternal damnation.

"I said: Behave." Raven's command shatters the darkness. The creature on her dais of women recoils.

"That's right! You do what you're told!" She taunts. She'll blame her behavior on the Alpha's life energy.

She rushes forward to the woman in the pentacle, burning through the bindings in quick succession. The weight of the girl is nothing in the shadow realm, but Khaylia needs to take the girl's body with her as well. She closes her eyes and reaches through the veil, tearing it until the facade of the house flits to life like a magic mirror.

Scooping the collapsed body into her arms she breaks the laws of reality to pull the body into the shadow.

No! You cannot have her!

"What are you going to do, stop me?"

Khaylia wraps an arm around the girl's waist, smirks, and kicks off like she's running the fifty yard dash at the Olympics. Moving at the speed of thought, she plows into the radiant light of her anchor, sandwiching the girl between her and Billy.

"Miss G." Billy's voice rasps as he catches her.

Magic always has a price and Khaylia's tab is coming due. She sways, watching Raven rush to check the Belmont girl and Billy.

"Don't worry about me," she waves her hand. "I'm fucking fine. Thanks."

Khaylia collapses.

CHAPTER TWENTY-NINE

Staking My Claim

Every inch of my body tingles with the need for more. Another orgasm, harder cocks, faster pumping. My soul cries in shrieking panic against the violation of my body, and is drowned by my need for adoration.

As if the universe heard my soul's plea, the invasion stops. The overwhelming erotic desire transforms to a warm embrace of life, burning every hint of lust and sadistic desire into ashes, leaving me cold and alone in the dark.

My senses return at a snail's pace.

The sweet scent of Billy Coeh's cologne envelopes me like a safety blanket. I'm panting as I try to reconcile my surroundings. I was kneeling in the pentacle, reciting the spell. Gracey's perfect voice chorusing mine. We were inside the house. Now I'm outside, and I'm naked. And sticky.

My throat is dry and scratchy, and my entire body trembles

like I ran a marathon twice over. My legs are sticky with my own juices. Shame burns hot against my cheeks as I cling to the massive arms holding me cradling me.

The most beautiful rumble comes from above me.

"Miss G?"

"Billy?" Disbelief that he could save us from that hell makes me afraid of what I'll see when I meet those dark brown eyes.

"Yes ma'am. You're alright. I got you." His brilliant smile, albeit weary, is a Godsend, and his eyes are kind as he inspects me.

"Sit down, honey. I need to check on the mage."

Billy calling someone a mage makes no sense to me. Gracey's not a mage. She's a siren. Like a small child, I stay where Billy puts me, hugging my knees to my chest to hide my nakedness.

He kneels next to the unconscious woman on the ground. Her auburn hair verifies she's not Gracey. Relief and panic slam into me.

Where is Gracey?

Whoever the woman is, she's not responding to his voice. Blood trickles from her nose. Billy settles on the ground, pulling the woman into his lap. He brushes her hair from her face before he cleans the blood away.

"Come on Miss Danakar, I need you to wake up." His gentle voice and soft shaking coaxes her to rouse.

Movement catches my eye, causing me to rock and hug myself tighter. I was hoping it was Gracey, but it's Raven staggering back from the house.

She's in pajamas and her hair sticks out in frizzy, wild curls. Her psycho witch vibe is amplified by the angry grimace on her face.

She kneels down on the other side of the unconscious woman.

"You can't sleep," she grumbles and rests her fingers on the woman's head.

"Gracey?" My voice is small as I call for her. My throat burns like I swallowed shards of glass.

No answer.

"Gracey!?" I scramble up and ignore the sharp rocks on the soles of my bare feet. I look at each person again, looking for her telltale blue hair.

"Gracey!" I shout into the night, my eyes darting in every direction for her.

Nathaniel! Where's Gracey?

Silence.

I freeze, my hands out as if I'm balancing on a ledge. I had gotten so used to him being ever-present that the void of his absence leaves me cold and vulnerable.

"What? No! What have I done?" Tears roll down my cheeks. I gulp for air. My lungs are on fire and my throat constricts. I stumble toward the house and stop, turning to see if Gracey appears. "Nathaniel, please. Gracey!" My scream is lost in my inability to breathe. I can't see from how hard I'm sobbing and I can't stop shaking. My legs won't work.

My head whips to the side and stars burst in my eyes with the ferocity of being slapped.

"Georgina, get a hold of yourself." Raven's sharp words pierce the hurricane of my panic. "You survived. All will be as it should be." She squeezes my shoulders. "Lia, where's the book?" she asks without looking away from me.

"Are you fucking serious? There was no fucking book." The other woman's voice is raspy and weak. "You're all fucking lucky I could grab blondie here! Shadow-walking isn't a game. She was being held by an Elder God! Do you even understand what that means?"

I jerk free of Raven and stumble to the other woman. Clinging to her. "Did you see Gracey?"

"What's a Gracey?" She pushes me off of her.

"She's my mate!" I shriek.

"Your what?" Billy turns me to focus on him, his eyebrows draw into a line, wrinkling his forehead. "What do you mean 'mate'?"

"Exactly what I said, Billy. She's my mate. We went in the house together to fix this and set Nathaniel free!"

The three of them exchange stern glances as if they're having an argument I'm not privy to.

"Don't look at me like that! There were three things in the shadow. Tentacles, Orgies, and this idiot." Khaylia growls as she throws her hands up in defense.

"This ain't good, Raven. If she has a siren and the book. She may not need Georgina anymore." Billy rubs his hand over his face.

"No," Raven waves a hand to dismiss the notion. "She cannot use the siren the same way without angering Poseidon. Even the Elder Ones respect the Gods. She wants back into this realm, not to end her existence."

I hate it when people treat me like I am still a child and talk like I'm not standing next to them.

"You mean this chick's mated to a siren and the two of them were in there doing who knows what to wake an Elder One? I thought you said she was a Belmont. Aren't they hunters? Not witches." Khaylia jerks her thumb at me.

Their bickering fades into the background as I move with renewed determination toward the house. If Gracey's still in there, I'm getting her back. I don't have time to stand around and listen to them bitch like a sewing circle.

A vice-grip clamps onto my arm and yanks me back around to face Raven.

"If all you are going to do is tell me to calm down, then let me the fuck go and get off my property! I will save Gracey myself. Even if I have to burn this fucking house to the ground!" My voice reaches a fever pitch and I shove Raven.

Her grip remains true, and her stare singes my soul.

The hot, muggy air swirls, howling in protest.

"You claim this land as yours?"

"Yes, it's my fucking house! I bought it!"

Unphased by my hysterics, Raven holds my gaze with her weird witchy eyes. "Answer me this, foolish girl. Do you risk everything for love?"

There is no hesitation in my heart. "I do."

"Will you forever seek to protect that which you love most?"

"How many fucking times do I have to tell you yes? Let me the fuck go!"

"Then by these questions three, I bind thee. May the heart of your love forever guide and shelter you. May you find that which you seek. May you ever be victorious in your quest to protect." Her words boom like she's wearing a microphone.

The earth shakes under us.

I fall to my knees. My vision blurs, forcing me to close my eyes. My skin tightens like I'm sunburned. Followed by the goose fleshing of being cold enough my teeth chatter. If I thought tentacles raping me was the worst feeling I ever experienced, I was mistaken. The whiplash of hot and cold makes me dry heave. My fingers curl and dig into the gravel of the driveway beneath me.

"What have you done to me?" I croak as I glare up at Raven.

"What you need."

"We stand with you."

"We can guide you."

"Save us."

I push to my feet, my muscles twitch from overuse, my head pounds like a drum core, and my heart cries for losing both Gracey and Nathaniel. I can't deal with Raven's cryptic bullshit anymore and turn my back to her with every intention of storming the castle and saving the princess from this psycho sex dragon.

The floating shades of men dot the lawn between me and the house. Their voices chant and echo as each one pledges to aid me on my quest.

My battered soul renews with the vigor of their support. One foot in front of the other, I move into the path they create, like they're the Red Sea and I'm Moses.

"Miss G," Billy whines.

"No, Billy. I'll never forgive myself if you get hurt too," I say without looking back.

"She's right, big fella. The Elder One can't stop her from entering. She can stop you. 'Sides. You go in there and succumb to her weird fuckfest then what? Think of what she could do with your Alpha abilities." Khaylia chimes in.

I leave the three of them behind and press forward. Each step closer I grow more confident in facing the monster in my mansion.

The house trembles at my touch. A terrible, heavy feeling cloaks me, drowning out all the voices.

I turn the handle and push open the door without an ounce of hesitation.

CHAPTER THIRTY

Choose Wisely

I stand in the foyer looking at the scorch marks and lanterns for a clue as to what to do next. No matter the consequences, I will not let Gracey and Nathaniel go. Too much time was wasted on chasing Richard. Now, I'll be damned if some sex-crazed demon is going to steal my only chance at happiness from me.

No tentacles or monsters greet me. The little copper bowls are cracked. Their goblin-dancing flames extinguished. The book is nowhere to be found. The lanterns are toppled over like bowling pins. No signs of Gracey or Nathaniel.

This house is too large to just pick a direction and wander. How will I ever find them?

In the doorway to the library, Nathaniel appears.

"Nathaniel!" Oh God, he's not a ghost. He's here in the flesh. He's a real person. My chest heaves as I stare at the man I've been bound to for the past three months.

He's like a statue staring through me.

"Nathaniel?" I step toward him.

He turns and walks into the library.

"Don't go!"

He stops, but does not turn back.

I'm alone in my skin. No pressing body parts. No shoulder taps. No emotions that are the complete opposite of mine.

I take another glance around the foyer, afraid of following him further in the house. "Stop being such a coward, Georgie. For once in your life, fight!"

I gulp and walk into the library.

Once lined with immaculate bookcases decorated with ornate trim, my heart aches to see the state it's in. Tonight, a bomb exploded here, leaving a gaping hole that leads to a creepy stone passageway. The shattered wood forms a clean path. Purple flames dancing from ancient sconces on the walls illuminate every detail of the passage.

Nathaniel stops, blocking the way into the passage and turns to face me again. Sorrow etches his handsome face as he lowers his gaze.

"What's down there? Is that where Gracey is? Is that where you are? Why can't I feel you?" I close the distance between us, hoping it brings back any hints of his warmth and comfort.

Saying nothing, he cups my cheek and smiles such a forlorn smile it breaks my heart.

A shiver runs through me like someone dumped a bucket of ice water on me; nothing like the loving embraces he gave me before.

Georgina.

My name echoes from a million miles away, and his anguish will haunt me for the rest of my days.

He motions with his free hand and leads me down the spiraling path.

The smooth concrete under my bare feet is surprisingly warm.

I fear this is a nightmare, not reality with how long this passage is. Have we been walking for minutes or hours? The walls are unchanging, and Nathaniel continues forward without looking back. This depressing parade never ends.

I reach the bottom and am greeted by a gaudy entry way. Carved around the opening are the same symbols from the book. Gold fills every crevice to excess. The room within casts a red glow, the only light down here, like a bloody fog blanketing the floor.

Without word or warning, Nathaniel evaporates from my side.

Fear paralyzes me. What if I can't save them? What if I get Gracey killed? What if I deserve whatever this woman wants with me?

Welcome, vessel.

Her voice is sweet and tantalizing, like a mother welcoming her prodigal daughter home.

Compelled to move, I enter the chamber.

Torches flare to life, bathing it in golden light to chase the bloody red, creating a campfire effect.

Two altars stand at the end of the room. Laying upon one is Nathaniel, naked with a jeweled dagger floating above his chest. On the other, displayed like Sleeping Beauty, lies Gracey, a similar dagger above her.

Eager to free them I rush forward.

When the shadow of a woman appears between them, I skid to a halt. Only her silhouette is visible. Trying to focus on her makes the mist ripple around her, like tentacles waving in water.

The time is nigh. You must choose.

The cursed book I should have never touched sails through the air and lands at my feet, opened to the same pages I had read from upstairs. When it touches the ground, the pentacle ignites, burning into the concrete, and tiny copper pots flare to life.

Dread twists my stomach. I want to vomit. I was a fool to think it could save any of us. Nathaniel warned me. Gracey warned me. Hell, even Raven warned me and I was too arrogant to listen. I read the pages, and all I saw was freedom. It was never freedom for Nathaniel. It was for the monster before me. "You want me to sacrifice one of them to set you free."

Complete the ritual. It's your destiny. Take what you desire most.

The whispered words tantalize my ears like a lover's sonnet.

"If I refuse?"

Ethereal screams rip through the room as thousands of tortured souls cry out in rage. Tentacles, sharp as razors, tear into my flesh.

Then you all die! I have waited this long and can wait longer. You are insignificant.

Her voice booms in a thunderous clap, silencing the screams.

I am not without mercy, my vessel. Do what your destiny demands, and I will give you all that your heart desires. You will live with the mate you choose for all eternity.

My brave facade cracks. I cover my mouth as the tears flow. My gaze dances between the two on the altars.

Oh, Gracey, Nathaniel. What have I done?

"What have I done?" A mocking singsong asks over my right.

I twirl to face whoever is standing next to me and see only carved cavern walls.

"What do I do?" This question comes from my left.

I jerk back to come face to face with a petite woman.

She barely stands five feet tall and her flowing brown hair ripples around her heart-shaped face. The white robe she wears ripples of its own accord. She flickers from the form of a woman to shadows. What frightens me most are the endless inky voids sprinkled with specs of starlight where her eyes should be.

I recoil.

The chiming laughter echoes off the chamber walls, magnifying as it repeats. Until it all stops as quickly as it started.

The familiar sensation of tendrils coiling around my waist and back forces me off my feet and pulls me back to her.

Tentacles writhe and dance in place of her dress.

"Who…" I have to swallow hard, my mouth dry. "Who are you?"

"Wrong question, vessel." She wags her finger as a coy smile dances over her face.

"What are you?"

"Still the wrong question." Her lips twitch with the hint of amusement.

The tentacles tighten, slithering over my skin.

The crushing weight of panic threatens to send me into a blubbering mess. I had held a sliver of hope there was another way out of this horrific nightmare. Completing the ritual is the only path out.

Maybe I can stall while I think of a way to save all of us. "What is it you desire?"

Her tentacles stop moving, holding me in place. She cants her head to a degree that would break a human's neck. When she rights herself, she flashes me a broad, wicked smile, revealing her fang-like teeth.

"You are the most amusing vessel."

My knees buckle.

She allows me to sink to the ground in front of the book. The tentacles whirl through the air, like vultures waiting for their prey to realize they are dead.

"What I desire is for you to finish the ritual. Do that, and you will live happily ever after. You will be loved most, and no one will ever hurt or abandon you again." Her tone is child-like, like she asked Santa to bring her a doll.

The tentacles vanish.

She floats and bobs, like she's skipping, to between the altars. Her fingers brush Nathaniel and Gracey's cheeks as she stares back at me.

"Isn't that what you desire? To be loved? I am even gracious enough to let you keep the beloved of your choice." Her giggle is sharp and grating. "Defy me again and not only will I make you suffer, I will use both of them to lure my next vessel to me. I have waited this long for freedom; I can wait longer still. You, little shepherd, have little time to choose."

Goosebumps prickle along my spine. My blood chills at the ice in her tone. She sounds playful in her threat, as if all of this is entertainment for her boredom.

Slimy creepy-crawly sensations run over my body, reminding me how easy it would be for her to destroy me. My heart hammers in my chest.

I gaze at the book. To complete the ritual, I have to sacrifice a soul.

Indecision plagues my heart and stays my hand.

How stupid I was. I was sacrificing Gracey upstairs without even realizing what I was doing. The spell was sucking her soul from her.

Tears drip from the tip of my nose onto the pages below. How can I choose to murder either of them?

Bile rises in the back of my throat. A niggling sensation of knowing this ritual is incorrect on all fronts creeps in.

I look up from the page at Gracey, only where she once was, an ethereal creature sleeps.

Sharp golden claws tip each of her fingers and toes. Tiny heel spikes jut out the back of each foot. Delicate soft feathers shimmer in sapphire blues and emerald greens over her forearms and shins, fading into skin at her thighs and upper arms. Delicate, bristling, dark-blue feathers crown her head before giving way to the long blue hair. Bunched and folded between her arms and body are wings covered in dazzling feathers.

My breath catches. The shock of seeing her in this form causes me to flinch and shut my eyes tight. I hate myself for reacting this way.

After several deep breaths, I calm enough that I can open my eyes to look at Nathaniel. His body is preserved and flush with life. His chest rises and falls as though he were in a slumber, and not dead for hundreds of years. No hint of rot, or sickness touches his naked skin.

"He's alive?"

"Of course! What good would a corpse do me?"

Her belittling laugh causes the hair on the back of my neck to rise, like hackles. If he isn't dead, how could he have possessed me?

Maybe what he thought was true, that his soul was being kept here by bonding with another. That would explain how he had survived all these years.

Raven said what happened to one happened to the other. Which means if I chose Gracey, then I have to sacrifice Nathaniel. If I sacrifice Nathaniel, then what happens to me?

I expect the woman-creature to taunt me.

She watches my struggle with bated breath.

I swallow my fear and place my hands on the book.

"May God forgive me for what I'm about to do."

Her cackling laughter rings in my ears as I focus on the pages below.

CHAPTER THIRTY-ONE

Complete the Ritual

I hate myself for being this weak. My life has been a winding road of bad decisions and regret. What a fool I was to think I could read a book and magically fix all my problems. Richard's hateful words rattle in my head like a snake ready to strike.

The compulsion to obey weighs me down against the book as I chant.

You're pathetic. Not even your old man wants you. You deserve to be her little slut. No one will ever love you.

"No!" I scream as I shake my head, trying to escape my mind. The words are the violent gibberish from before.

"I will always love you, Georgie."

The sweet Georgia drawl of my mother banishes Richard's abusive words into oblivion.

Momma?

******

"I will always love you, Georgie." My mother wipes away the tears from my puffy red cheeks with my father's silky hanky as she squats in front of me.

"I want Daddy to love me!" I wail, my pigtails bobbing as I stomp my foot.

"Oh, honey, of course he loves you. Whatever made you think he doesn't?"

"He didn't buy me Elmo!" My world is ending because I do not possess the fluffy red doll.

We had gone to fetch my brother a birthday present when I saw the doll on the shelf. My father had not deigned it important to obtain me a toy as well, and this is unforgivable. My father suffered my wrath the entire way home and fled as soon as my mother rescued him from me.

"Georgie," she says in the same tone she uses when she catches me sneaking cookies.

I double down with the crocodile tears and stomp my foot again.

"Georgina." Her voice sharpens and her hands rest on her hips.

I've pushed too far. I draw in dramatic breaths coupled with sniffles to calm down. "Momma," I whine.

"This trip was for your brother. It is okay to not get a new toy every time you go to the store."

"It was Elmo! He was mine!"

"Georgina Rae Belmont." Her soft smile and soothing tone are replaced with a frown and my name spoken like the crack of a whip. "No, he wasn't yours. Just because you wanted Elmo does not make him yours."

I shuffle my feet, ashamed that I made Momma mad. "It's not fair! Tyler gets a new toy, and I don't."

Momma sighs and raises her hand to her forehead. "I know! Life is so unfair."

I giggle at her dramatics.

"Georgie, you're always telling me you are a big girl, and life isn't always fair to big girls. There is one thing that I know to be true and unchanging."

"What's that?" My sniffles are almost all dried. I wipe snot from my nose with the back of my hand.

"That your father and I love you. We always have. We always will."

"How do you know?"

"Because I always bring you chocolate milk." My father walks into the room.

His familiar deep baritone causes a complete one-eighty in my attitude. I break into a smile. All the waterworks vanish as I see the plastic cup in his hand. I squeal in delight and rush over to steal the cup from his grip.

"Like your mom said, jellybean, I'm always going to love you. It was in the contract I signed." He scoops me up into his strong and warm embrace. "In the fine print. Article III: Thou shalt forever love your daughter!"

His exaggerated hand motions as he pretends to read makes me giggle again.

******

My heart aches at the memory.

Why did he stop loving me the way he did then?

Moment after moment slap the self-loathing pity party out of me.

My father when he pulled me from the closet. His hand

sprawled against the back of my head as he held my face buried against his chest.

The two of us traveling all the way to London, while he gives me everything I ask for along the way.

His beaming, proud smile when I graduated high school, then college.

Every moment he let me rant and rave like a violent storm, while he remained the silent, steady anchor.

How he helped me get and renovate my apartment, despite wanting me to live with him at the estate.

Gracey would always tell me he didn't hate me.

Nathaniel said the same thing.

Richard had fueled the fire of resentment, pointing out all the ways I was a disappointment to him and to my father, re-affirming that is why he didn't love me.

Georgina Belmont!

Momma's stern reprimand echoes and fades through my mind once more when I let Richard's abuse slip back in.

My eyes focus and in my hand is the dagger that hovered over Nathaniel while I still kneel at the book.

When did I get the dagger?

I had stopped chanting and am held poised like a murderous psycho over the book.

My pulse slows, and my body relaxes. The compelling force to obey no longer holds me hostage.

Finish it, vessel!

I taught you better than this, young lady.

Momma stands before me, her hands on her hips and the blue glow around her blocks the terrifying monster demanding I set her free.

What are you waiting for? Don't you want to spend eternity with your precious Gracey?

The woman taunts. Her voice muted by the shield of my mother.

Do what must be done, Georgina.

Her hand rests on my shoulder.

The chains of blissful ignorance shatter and I gasp.

A surge of energy whips my soul into a frenzy. Repressed power spreads from deep within me until every nerve is alive with the magic I possess.

The monster was not wrong.

I am a shepherd, a soul mage, a link between this world and the ones beyond.

Knowledge is power, and my mother is making me invincible.

I can control the veil. I don't need a book of spells, or a sacrifice.

All the voices flood back as they scream for me to close the veil. To save them from an eternal damnation of this monster's reign.

My mother smiles down at me as she dissipates.

The monster before me fills every inch of this room. Tentacles whip through the air as her eyes burn like two fiery orbs where the starry voids once were.

You are not alone.

The voices chorus all around us.

I had foolishly thought that opening the veil was how you set Nathaniel's soul free from mine.

He tried to warn me, but I didn't listen.

Now I realize this beast has been controlling both of us the entire time.

"You know what I most desire?" I shout. "For you to crawl back under the rock you came from and leave us the fuck alone!"

The dagger clanks against the floor.

It screeches and the room trembles, threatening to come crashing down.

As it enters the pentacle, the bloody seal burns with fire.

I slam the book closed.

Words flow from my mouth. The fever-pitched Gregorian chant rings against her shrieks.

I have been baptized into this world of monsters. Fear and doubt no longer plague me.

Tentacles flail and whip me, drawing blood.

The stale stench of old sex and mildew fades away to be replaced with the revitalizing scent of freshly fallen rain and wildflowers.

The souls' voices raise in a gospel chorus as the words escape my lips.

No longer the girl who wouldn't be loved, I square my shoulders and stand tall. I am a Belmont, a monster hunter, and I will defend all that I love until I draw my last breath.

No! You are my vessel!

A heavy blow lands on my back, threatening to snap my spine. Searing pain flares to life in my chest. My breath hitches and all of my willpower goes into remaining standing.

Her dark tendril splits and slithers against me. Everywhere it touches me, welts form. The hunting tendrils replicate and slither until they are threatening to swallow me whole.

The excruciating pain is nothing like I have never experienced. Darkness encroaches on my vision. The crushing tentacles that have broken through whatever barrier had been protecting me. My mother's warmth and strength obliterated.

Valiant effort, vessel.

The creature sneers at me, her tentacles rising like a black curtain of death.

You have defied me for the last time.

This can't be the end. I'm supposed to win. The heroes always win.

The warmth in my soul flutters. The candle flame of my power threatens to extinguish in the wind of her dark energy. The tentacles compress tighter around my chest, making my words pinched and strangled.

"Breathe." A strange, feminine voice commands my body to function.

Air floods into my lungs. Raspy words flow forth, sound returns to the chant.

My body shakes at the sudden release and I gulp air between the words I shout.

Another ear-piercing screech echoes through the cavern.

Standing around the ring and altars are several young women, hand-in-hand like a shield. Dark tentacles whip and violate them. Their shield holds true, like an ethereal game of Red Rover. They prevent the creature from punching through. Each young woman holds her head high and in their protection I am granted a moment's reprieve. Flashes of light burst like lightning with each tentacle that bombards their blockade.

The one who spoke stands across from me is dressed like one of those Civil War re-enactors. Her youthful gaze looks upon the unconscious Nathaniel cradled in her arms. The soft smile and tenderness in her gaze shows me her love for him.

"He always was earnest and kind. My dear husband."

I recall an old black-and-white photograph that I had found in my research. She's Delores, the first victim of Haven Hill. Her family had taken over this plantation after Sherman's march to the sea razed it.

Nathaniel had said she was special. That his connection with her was almost as deep as the one he had felt with me.

"I was like you." Her melancholy voice is whisper thin. "I was a vessel. One with the ability to finish that which the Followers of S'heol'g'orah f-"

The world twists as she says that name, like I'm strapped into one of those carnival rides that flips you upside down as it spins in a circle.

The monster roars above us.

What the fuck is a S'heol-

"Do not dare to even think of her name!" Delores stares at me. "Her control over you is tenuous still. I am already bound to her. Using her name can do little to me. You are still free from her control. You cannot let her win. With your power, she will destroy everything. Her lust is insatiable. She's a cruel Master. You must sever all her connections to this realm."

She returns her attention to Nathaniel.

I follow her gaze, her words stab me in the heart.

He is the monster's link to this world, a crack in the prison it desires freedom from.

I can shut the veil and lock her away. If I don't break her hold on him, she will use him again.

Everything halts, as if a person pushed pause on the horror movie I'm living.

How did this fucking dagger get back in my hand?

Nathaniel kneels before me, his boyish smile greeting my tearful gaze.

"Hi." He gives me a small wave.

"Hi," I laugh at the brevity he brings in this terrifying moment.

His lips are soft as he draws me into a tender kiss.

He's everything I wanted Richard to be. How could I murder this beautiful, kind man?

The dagger weighs heavy in my hand as he nuzzles me and pulls me closer. His lips trail along my chin and he nibbles my neck.

Lust blossoms and I want his touch like a greedy junky seeking my next fix.

I nuzzle him and draw his lips back into another sweet kiss.

"I love you, Georgina."

"I forgive you, Nathaniel." murmured against his lips as I plunge the dagger into his chest. I'm too much of a coward to look him in the eyes as I murder him.

He gasps.

Instead of pulling away he holds me tighter and rests his forehead against mine. "Thank you," he whispers.

Molten lines spider along the dagger, and it shatters in my grip. Shrapnel pierces my skin.

Light blazing as bright as the sun chases every inch of evil away.

What have you done? No!

Inky darkness enshrouds S'heol'g'orah. Her shrieks fade as a grasping hand pulls her back to the depths of whatever hell she belongs to.

Nathaniel is gone.

All the brides are gone.

I am alone in a silent tomb.

I clutch my bleeding and marred hand as the sharp sting of a blade rips through my chest. Shaking and curling into a ball as I fall over.

I hope Gracey finds someone after I'm gone.

My eyes flutter closed.

CHAPTER THIRTY-TWO

Home Sweet Home

"I know you hate it, Isaiah." Mehzebeen says.

"I should be helping her."

Abandoning her at the mansion was the second hardest choice he had to make in his life. He regrets getting into this Mercedes to face the music of his actions.

"The Collector was explicit in his demands."

"Fucking Collector," I grumble.

This is why the first rule of being a hunter is to never make a deal of any kind with the Fae. Once such a powerful being holds sway, it is near impossible to go against their wishes.

The Collector had issued a bounty on Isaiah and his family. He called it a 'breach of contract' and took Isaiah's decision to tell his daughter the truth as an insult.

Georgina was having night terrors after her brother attacked her. He made a Devil's bargain with the man. The Collector took away the anguish she felt at losing her mother and brother. In exchange, Isaiah agreed to abandon being a hunter. He found wiggle room in the agreement by becoming the human advisor to the Council. As long as Georgina remained in the dark regarding the underworld, the Collector looked the other way.

There are always consequences to undoing Fae magic. Isaiah chose to tell her what he had done, thinking those consequences wouldn't come back to bite him, or Georgina as soon as they did. He had assumed that the mighty Isaiah Belmont, hunter extraordinaire, could fend them off and protect her forever.

The boy was killing her.

His assumption of who Nathaniel was and how he came to be linked to Georgina was enough leverage to even cause The Collector to take pause. That Fae prick denied any such accusations of him violating the contract first as he agreed to my terms.

"I would do it all over again," Isaiah confesses to Mehzebeen.

"Which is even more reason to abide by this new agreement, Isaiah."

"Doesn't mean I have to like it," he mutters as he stares out the window.

"That is a sign it was a compromise. I seem to recall Lincoln saying something to that effect once."

"Hrmph." Isaiah hates when she's right.

For six hours, he has been held prisoner in this car. He should be fighting by her side, protecting her. She doesn't know anything. How will she defeat a God damn Elder God?

"She is stronger than you give her credit for," Mehzebeen's soft reproach draws a glare from Isaiah.

The Mercedes pulls into Haven Hill, rolling to a stop not far from the trio of people clustered in front of the house.

"Where is she?" Isaiah shouts as she leaps from the slowing car and storms toward the small group of people staring at the house.

"Mr. Belmont?" Billy turns to face Isaiah.

"Mehzebeen," his surprised tone turns icy as he greets the vampire.

"Where is Georgina? Is she alive?" Isaiah yells at them, cutting off whatever pissing contest lingers between vampire and werewolf.

He looks from one person to the next, desperate for the answer.

Billy, the man he entrusted to protect Georgina when he couldn't, lowers his gaze, unable to answer.

The auburn-haired woman won't meet his gaze.

He narrows his eyes as he doesn't recognize her and he knows everyone in Savannah who's anyone.

The more he tries to focus on her, the worse she fidgets.

Frustrated he shifts his gaze to Raven. "Madame, where is she?" His voice cracks with fear that his daughter is dead.

Her head's canted, like she's listening to someone explaining instructions.

He does not further interrupt her while she communicates with the spirits.

"I see." She nods her head and her lips curl into a smile. "Isaiah, everything is as it should be."

"Isaiah," Mehzebeen draws his attention to the mansion.

The looming, ever-present shadows lift from around the massive building. The heavy and dreary air lightens. The silence fades as crickets and frogs chirp their normal night noises. With the dark and foreboding vibe gone, the house looks like a run-down shell.

Isaiah bolts across the lawn. He must find Georgina. She has to be alive.

Air burns his lungs as he bursts inside.

Mehzebeen and Billy are hot on his tail and the three freeze at the scene in the foyer.

The pentacle scorches the tile, leaving the magnificent floors cracked and broken. The remains of copper bowls lie in pieces. Camp lanterns cast eerie shadows where they lie.

"Georgina!" Isaiah head whips back and forth as he searches for any signs of her.

"This way, Mr. Belmont." Billy sniffs the air and motions for them to follow.

They rush into the library. Rubble lines the floor. A small path with tiny footprints leads to a hole in the wall. The air here is colder and staler.

Isaiah pushes by Billy and hurries into the tunnel, uncaring of what may lie in wait. If his little girl is in there, he'll face the Devil himself to save her.

The descent takes an eternity until we reach the bottom and come face to face with a buried Cathedral's entrance. The threshold is smeared with blood and grime over the intricate gold.

All Isaiah can think is he's looking at what remains of his daughter, and he shakes his head.

A wailing cry inside makes the three of them rush through the threshold.

Gracey sits cradling Georgina's limp body and sobs against her.

Isaiah drops his knees next to Gracey and tries to pry Georgina from her grasp.

"No," she hisses and clings tighter.

"Sophia Grace, please," he begs.

"Isaiah, let me." Mehzebeen's soft hand rests on his shoulder.

He pauses and breaks the second rule taught to hunters by looking her square in the eyes.

Looking into a vampire's eyes is a dangerous proposition at the best of times. He needs to trust her to save his little girl. Easing back, he hovers over the three women, worse than a buzzing bee over a hive.

"Release her," Mehzebeen commands.

Gracey hisses again before her arms go lax, and Mehzebeen eases Georgie from her grasp.

His hands clench into fists and his weight shifts with the readiness to tackle Mehzebeen away from Georgina if she so much as puts one fang near her skin. Vampires are not known for healing people and if Georgina is already dead, the only way to bring her to life is to turn her.

A massive hand clamps on his shoulder, keeping him in place. "She will not hurt her, Isaiah." Alpha Coeh's tone is low and soothing. His grip does not loosen when Isaiah tries to shake him off.

Mehzebeen's words are firm and echo in this cathedral. Ancient Egyptian slips from her lips like a bubbling brook. Golden light balls in her palm and paints a sunny glow over Georgina's skin.

Soon the sounds of bones cracking back into place and Georgina's chest rises and falls.

Her raspy, gurgling breaths are music to Isaiah's ears.

He had always known Mehzebeen was a Bride of Lucifer, and that it gifted her more powers than usual vampires. This is beyond what he imagined. That kind of power doesn't look like the gift of Satan. He doesn't care, it saved his baby.

As she staggers away from Georgina, Alpha Coeh releases

Isaiah, and he rushes forward. "Georgie?"

******

"Daddy?" My eyes flutter open. I had accepted my fate and knew that by murdering Nathaniel I murdered myself. Is this what heaven looks like? The love and concern of my father?

Gracey flings herself against me, sobbing.

My father pulls us into a tighter hug, causing me to whimper.

"Shh… It's okay. I'm here. I got you, baby girl." he kisses my temple before he turns his head to look at something.

I'm being smothered by Gracey's affection to see what he's looking at.

"She couldn't stay. We should get the girls out of here." Billy's voice floats above me.

What is he doing in heaven? I left him outside.

My father takes off his suit jacket and wraps it around me as he scoops me up.

The jacket is warm and the safety of his scent wraps like a cocoon around me. I curl into him as he carries me.

"Billy, make sure that damnable place is packed full of concrete."

"Yes, sir."

We emerge from the house.

My father's straining from carrying me all the way out.

As much as I don't want to leave the safety of his arms, I squirm to stand on my own.

He hesitates before he nods and sets me down.

I lean against him, and he puts his arm around me.

Raven and Khaylia are bickering like an old married couple.

Gracey appears by my side, swallowed by Billy's T-Shirt.

255

Gone are the feathers and claws, replaced with the woman I love.

My father shifts to rest his hand on Gracey's shoulder, holding us both against him.

The four of us watch in silence.

"No! There is more to do," Madame scolds.

"Listen! I'm tired as fuck. Dat hunter ain't gonna be no good for either of us iffn he figures me out. What's there left to do?"

"Your Cajun is showing," Raven teases before whirling to face an unknown entity. "Yes, yes. They need to make up. Woman! I swear, if you had let me talk to him from the start, we wouldn't be in this mess. No! You don't get to pop in whenever you want! I'm not a public telephone!"

Dad clears his throat.

"Fuck me, I want to go home," Khaylia throws her hands in the air.

"Lia. Shush," Raven growls as she faces us.

"Lia? As in Khaylia?" Dad asks.

She holds her hands up in defense. "I ain't done nothin' to ya, hunter! Don't burn me at the stake."

Raven snorts.

My dad chuckles. "I don't make a habit of burning women at the stake. Leaves an awful smell."

Billy snorts.

Khaylia looks from one face to the next, and takes a step back, like she's about to run away.

"Thank you," my father says. "For saving my daughter."

"What you playin' at, hunter?"

"No games. I owe you."

Her demeanor goes from long-tailed cat in a room of rocking chairs to smug asshole in no time flat. "You hear that, Raven? He owes me."

Raven rolls her eyes, then turns off to the side again. "Hold your horses! He's not going anywhere!"

Her body jerks like a bird on a wire. Her head lolls back before she snaps into normal posture and stares at me with clouded eyes.

"Isaiah, Georgina," Momma's voice echoes from Raven's mouth.

Daddy stiffens.

"Momma?"

"You are all each other has in this world. Isaiah, you must be her guide and mentor. Georgina, you must learn to trust yourself, and your father. I love you."

Raven collapses into Khaylia's arms.

Billy scoops her up. "You able to drive that thing?" He nods towards Raven's little Geo.

"Yeah. She gonna be alright?" Khaylia frowns at Raven.

"I'll see her home safe. I'm guessing she's worn out." Billy heads to his truck with Raven.

Khaylia takes one look at Isaiah and bolts for the car.

I wriggle free of my dad and curl into Gracey.

"I lost my keys," Gracey mumbles.

We stare at the house.

My breathing picks up and Gracey's shaking next to me.

"Wait here," my father says.

"No, Daddy," I whimper, but too afraid to follow him as he heads back into the house.

Gracey and I hold each other as we stare at the door.

What if that monster claimed him? What's taking him this long?

As I muster the courage to leave Gracey's hold and go after

him, he emerges, pulling the door closed behind him.

I exhale and retreat into the safety of Gracey's arms.

"Let's go home." He rattles the keys as he guides us to Gracey's car.

EPILOGUE

The Collector stands silent at the window of a small suburban house, watching the first rays of dawn peek over the horizon. He enjoys watching the way puny humans spend their time frolicking about, unaware of how fragile and fleeting their existence is.

The taste of bitter tea floods his mouth as he sips from the delicate porcelain cup in his hand. The one downside to having a vampire as a personal servant is the stench of death clings to them and everything around them. His smile twists and sours as he puts the cup back on the saucer and sets it on the end table.

"Did you get it?" His voice is deep and rich, full of the kind of danger that makes all the girls throw caution to the wind. As he speaks to his servant hovering near him it only holds irritation.

"Yes, Master."

The Collector strides from his window and through his collection. Glass curio after glass curio filled with dangerous and powerful artifacts line the space.

His servant lifts a small package, offering it to his Master.

The Collector looks at it like it was a viper ready to

strike.

"Oh, dear sister." He sighs as he takes the book.

She has always been a nuisance. Her essence quivers against the restraints of the closed cover. Her habit of going on walkabouts, as she calls them, was bound to cause him trouble. This time she went too far, interfering with his work.

He carries the tome to a special case, sequestered in a corner all of its own. Red velvet lines the bottom.

He fishes around in a vest pocket for a few moments before pulling out an ancient key. After sliding the tiny key into the intricate lock, he eases the glass cover open with care.

"You have been naughty. If you would be kind enough to stay where I put you this time, I might see to you being granted a reprieve from your sentence."

He appreciates that she cannot answer him as he sets the book into place. "You did well in grabbing the book before they could get to it."

The vampire preens under his praise.

The Collector wanders downstairs. A simple breakfast and a fresh pot of tea are all he needs after the previous evening's events.

He worries that should his sister get free, then it would summon his brother to this realm. While she will run roughshod over the humans, she does it only for her own amusement.

On the other hand, their brother is a cruel and exacting tyrant. He would seek to rule this realm as he does his own. Keeping him out of the picture is far better for humans than they could ever know.

Sweet jam sours in his mouth as he pauses chewing and lets the paper in his hands droop. His servant knows better than to disturb him while he enjoys toast and jam.

The Collector takes his time finishing the bite as he watches the young man squirm before him. Whatever happened in the few minutes it took to walk down the stairs has the boy terrified. "Spit it out already."

"Master, it's missing."

"What's missing?"

"The book, sir."

He abandons the food and paper, taking the stairs two at a time as he flies back to his study. How could she break the seal? He had re-bound the spell to hold her in place.

His breath is quick and ragged. By the time he slides to a halt in front of the case, his impeccable suit is disheveled. A quick check of his breast pocket reassures him the key is still in his possession.

With trembling fingers, he touches the case. The hum of his magic reverberates off his fingers, proving the ward is intact.

"This is unfortunate."

He stares at the empty spot in the red velum box where S'heol'g'orah's book of spells had been. He will never hear the end of it from his brother if he finds out. He was entrusted with keeping her in her prison for eons.

Now he lost her twice in two hundred years.

"Most unfortunate, indeed."

Biography

J. R. Froemling was born in Indiana, the second eldest of three. She met her first husband in an online writing community. She met her second husband at a board game convention in 2015. She has a Bachelor's of Science in Information Technology from Western Governors University of Indiana. She got her start in an online writing community for Star Wars fan fiction. Over the past twenty years she has transformed that love of fan fiction into works of her own.

https://jrfwriting.com

Other Books By J. R. Froemling

<u>Savannah Nights Series</u>
jrfwriting.com/books/savannah-nights/
The Triple Six
The Night Rangers

<u>The Wolfe Legacy</u>
jrfwriting.com/books/wolfe-legacy/
Mistress Giselle - Book One of Hope-Marie
A Devil's Hope - Book Two of Hope-Marie
The Naughty List - Book One of Elijah Joseph

<u>Chronicles of Nodd</u>
jrfwriting.com/books/chronicles-of-nodd/
Fall of Avalon - Verse One

<u>Immortal Love Saga</u>
jrfwriting.com/books/immortal-love-saga/
My Viking Alpha